# MIKE MARS IN ORBIT

*Other books in the Mike Mars Series:*

MIKE MARS ASTRONAUT

MIKE MARS FLIES THE X-15

MIKE MARS AT CAPE CANAVERAL

# Mike Mars in Orbit

## BY DONALD A. WOLLHEIM

DOUBLEDAY & COMPANY, INC.

GARDEN CITY, NEW YORK

1961

*Special Acknowledgment Notice*

The author wishes to extend his personal thanks for the valuable assistance rendered him in the course of preparing this book by the United States Air Force. In particular, thanks are due to Major James F. Sunderman, Chief of the USAF Book Program, to Major Kenton D. McFarland and Captain James C. Sparks, Jr., of the USAF Information Office in New York, and to Major Kenneth E. Grine and his staff at Patrick Air Force Base.

# Contents

1. The Radar at Skyhook     13
2. No Way to Treat a Lady     25
3. Traitor's Trail     36
4. Shadow on the Stars     42
5. Wire by Wire, Bolt by Bolt     50
6. The Voice of Trouble     58
7. On Your Mark, Get Set!     66
8. Four Go North     76
9. Killer Countdown     86
10. Substitute Hero     96
11. "Bermuda Reports . . ."     105
12. "T Minus Zero"     113
13. "Go, Mike, Go!"     123
14. Quicksilver One     132
15. The Green Tube     141
16. The Silent Satellite     148
17. Decision at Canaveral     157
18. Point of Re-Entry     162
19. The Pirates of Zanzibar     171
20. Half a World Away     181

MIKE MARS IN ORBIT

## CHAPTER 1

## THE RADAR AT SKYHOOK

THE September night was hot, humid, and especially dark for there was no moon. The stars looked down from a clear midnight sky, and their faint rays were the only illumination gleaming on the small lake at the estate called Skyhook.

The buildings around the lake were also silent and dark. A small porch light gleaming on the big old-fashioned southern building that housed the astronauts, and one or two hooded lights outside the entrances of the low buildings that housed the workshops and laboratories of the secret setup were the only lights to be seen.

In the thick central Florida woods that surrounded the isolated estate there were some sounds and motions—the noises of little animals, the stirring of lizards, the faint hiss of a snake. Life never entirely slept in these woods. But there was one thing moving through the trees that was different that night.

A human figure was slipping silently between the

trees, moving carefully to avoid bumping into things, sometimes shining a carefully hooded flashlight just enough to see if the trail was clear. Sometimes there was a muttered exclamation as the mysterious person became confused, or stepped into something that snagged the foot or clung to the clothing.

Slowly, carefully, this figure passed through the woods and finally came to a stop as the faint starlight now broke through the edge of the trees to reveal a high wire fence. This was the boundary of Skyhook; beyond was the destination the midnight visitor sought.

The figure paused, looked up and down the wire, then began to move silently along it, following the fence, examining it for a weak spot. As it moved, from somewhere on the other side of the wire a dark four-legged figure came out of the darkness. The prowler stopped short. The newcomer on the inside of the wire stopped also, then moved slowly, stiff-leggedly forward, and a low growling sound could be heard. One of the big watchdogs that prowled the wire at night had caught the scent of the stranger.

The unknown visitor reached into the darkness of its robes, withdrew something, and threw it over the wire. The thing, a little ball of raw meat, fell at the feet of the big dog. The dog gave a single loud bark, then sniffed it, and gobbled it down. The prowler waited in silence. The dog returned its attention to the stranger, resuming its faint growling. But in a few more minutes of this silent contest, the dog seemed to lose its air of suspicion and stopped its growling. In a moment, it turned as if forgetting the prowler, and slowly wagging its tail, began to amble away toward the distant shack that guarded the main gate.

Once again the prowler resumed the careful examination of the wire; at last stopping, the figure bent down.

There was a depression in the ground where once the shallow bed of a tiny stream had passed under the wire—and would do so again as soon as the next rains came. Right now it was dry, as the probing hand of the prowler determined.

The unknown person stopped, looked around carefully, peered through the wires. Beyond the open fields was Skyhook. The dim black outlines of the buildings could be seen far away against the star-strewn sky. Skyhook was large and there were many acres between that outer wire and the main grounds.

The prowler bent down, pressed close to the ground, squeezed into the bottom of the depression and crawled carefully under the wire. With a few muffled grunts and groans, scraping against the ground, it finally got under, pulled itself up to a sitting position, this time inside the wire, and finally got to its feet, panting a little breathlessly.

15

Hundreds of feet away from this point was the regular road that led into Skyhook. There was a gate there, now closed and locked, and a small shack in which a man was sitting at a desk, his seat tipped over, a small light shining over his shoulder as he read a book. This was the security man on duty that night, not in uniform, but still a member of the Air Force's special guard which had established a careful security patrol all around the very special base of America's top secret space flight project.

The guard was not aware that someone had gotten through the wire. It was so unlikely. Few people in the whole United States even knew of the project's existence. So far, no one had ever attempted the entry. So he was not to be blamed that this night the attempt had been made and had succeeded.

He had heard one of the watchdogs bark a little while before and had looked up. But in a moment he had seen the dog come from where it had barked, and he could see that it was not disturbed. It was ambling along, wagging its tail in the light from his shack window. Nothing was disturbing that hound now, the watchman thought, and resumed his reading.

The uninvited visitor turned away from the direction in which the watchhouse lay and began carefully walking in the direction of the nearest of the silent buildings.

Mike Mars sat up in bed. The room was dark and

he could hear the slow measured breathing of his roommate, Johnny Bluehawk, asleep in bed on the other side of the small bedroom. Mike strained his eyes around the room, making out in the darkness the dim shapes of the bureau and the wide window through which came the soft breath of the warm night air and the sounds of crickets and insects.

He looked around him. He was restless; he felt uneasy. Reaching over, he found his radium-dial watch on the night table, picked it up and looked at it: a few minutes after midnight. He and his fellow astronauts had retired early, as was their custom here. They believed in a good night's sleep making a good day's work. For an alert mind, rest and sleep were the best foundation.

Now something was wrong. He didn't know what, but he was sure somehow that something was strange. He half-remembered a dog that had barked. Probably that was what had awakened him. He looked around the room again, then finally slipped his legs out of bed, worked his feet into his shoes, and quietly laced them up over his pajama legs.

Careful as he was, the keen ears of his Indian comrade heard him. There was a sound from the other bed, then Johnny's voice, as sharp as if wide awake— which was the case. Johnny Bluehawk always woke up fully alert.

"What's up, Mike? Something doing?"

"I don't know," said Mike softly. "I just can't sleep. Thought I heard something. I was thinking of slipping out and taking a brief walk. Maybe I can determine what's bothering me, and set my mind at ease."

Johnny Bluehawk sat up in bed. "You're not worrying about going into orbit, are you? Or do you think Tench is going to get active again, now that we're working on the next phase of our program?"

Mike stood up, reached for his dark blue Air Force trenchcoat. "No, the orbit program doesn't worry me. I never cross bridges till I come to them. But you may have something there about Tench. They never did catch him, you know. We haven't had any trouble of that kind for a couple of months."

"Maybe you think it's time now," said Johnny. "I don't see how he'd dare come within a hundred miles of us."

Mike started toward the door. "You go back to sleep," he cautioned his fellow astronaut. "I'll be back in a little while. I'm just going to walk over to the radio shack, take a peek at the radar setup. There's a point about it that I want to clear up in my mind."

Johnny settled back into bed. "Don't wake the rest of the folks then."

"I won't," said Mike, and carefully opening the door, he stepped softly out, and closed it behind him. He made his way down the wide hall, past the doors

18

of the other young pilots who made up Project Quicksilver, and tiptoed down the wide curving stairs to the ground floor.

He gained the main door, opened it, and stepped out onto the porch. The bulb over the door shed a soft glow on him as he passed. He glanced at it with his gray eyes, then, turning away, ran a hand through his tousled shock of sandy hair and stepped down the stairs onto the damp grass. There was a faint breeze in the night air and he wrapped the trenchcoat about his pajamas. Its dark color made him almost invisible in the moonless night.

He walked softly across the grass, thinking as he went about the night and the stars and the work ahead. Project Quicksilver was the doorway to space for America, and he often thrilled to himself as to how lucky he had been to be there when it opened.

But it wasn't all adventure—in fact it had been actually study, hard work, and careful preparation all the way. Still, there was the promise of adventure. He had seen outer space.

Twice he'd been out there, out in the empty void beyond the air, out where the stars shone all the time and the sky was black and the planets waited for man's first footfall. Soon Mike knew he'd be going again.

But as he had told Johnny that wasn't what had awakened him. What had?

*Mike stepped out on the porch.*

He pondered this as he went. He looked up at the stars, he looked out across the silent sleeping grounds of the private estate which had been made the headquarters of this secret space group. Nothing moved, everything was apparently peaceful.

He reached the radio laboratory, and found the door locked. He reached into his trenchcoat pocket for the bunch of keys he'd taken from his pants pocket as he'd left the bedroom. Fingering them, he tried a couple until at last the door swung open.

He went into the radio building—a low structure which housed the equipment on which they practiced and the experimental models they might be using in outer space trips. He put on a low light near the door and walked over to one of the radar consoles.

He sat down at it, switched on its hooded light, then pressed the button which started the radar antenna on the roof to turning slowly on its axis so that it would survey the entire locality. He flicked on his radar screen.

The screen glowed a series of green dots, and the slowly circling arm of the radar eye brought into outline the crude indications of the Skyhook terrain. There was the outline of the main building; there the outlines of the outer laboratories; there the garages, there the private hangar out back where the landing strip lay. Now here came the patch of trees near the tennis courts, and this was the handball court. There beyond now came the line of the outer wire and the jumble that was the forest beyond. There was the line of the forest, and that was the road, and the gate and the guardhouse, all in flickering green dots, flaring up and then slowly fading away until the next sweep of the arm revived them.

There was the fence sweeping around to meet the lake, and . . . there was something moving. A dot in slow motion in the cleared space between the fence and the space capsule laboratory. Mike tensed over the console, studied it. There was something moving, something that had come from the wire and was heading for that building. It was small, but large enough to be man-sized.

Mike leaned back excited. This was what had been bothering him. There was an intruder on the grounds. He switched off the console of the radar, shut down the sweep of the roof antenna, slipped over to the wall, and switched off the light. He went to the door and looked in the direction of the capsule building.

Closing the door silently behind him, he moved off toward the capsule building, bent down, silent, hurrying to intercept the prowler. He realized as he went that he could have simply put in the alarm, and the guards would floodlight the area. But this was more personal.

He didn't want to chance the prowler making good

an escape. Mike had an ax to grind. During the course of his work, there had been several attempts on the astronauts—and directly at Mike himself.

This time perhaps he'd put his hands on the mysterious enemy. This chance he wouldn't let pass.

He hoped he had reached the other building before the stranger. He could see nothing yet, but he inched up beside the door and flattened himself against the side of the building.

*Mike waited for the prowler.*

Now he saw at last the dark figure of someone coming up. He heard the faint swish of wet grass beneath the intruder's feet. He waited a moment, and as the dark prowler reached the door, Mike jumped forward and grabbed the stranger hard in the old high-school tackle.

There was a sudden gasp and the two of them went down in a heap on the ground.

## CHAPTER 2

## NO WAY TO TREAT A LADY

Two voices broke the stillness of the night at the same instant. One was an utterly unexpected high-pitched feminine scream. The other was an equally astonished gasp from Mike Mars, "Hey! It's a woman!"

"Of course it's a woman, you big lummox," came from the sprawled body on the grass, now trying to get to its feet. Mike had untangled himself as fast as he could once he found himself mixed up in a mass of skirts and was also scrabbling to his feet. "That's no way to treat a lady!" came from the stranger in a quavering tone.

"I guess so, ma'am, but you hadn't ought to be wandering around here in the dead of night," said Mike defensively, now on his feet and helping the other to hers. "Besides, who are you anyway?"

When the stranger was on her feet—she was surprisingly small and light, Mike noticed—he kept a firm hold on her arm and escorted her across the grass

25

to the radio building. She was puffing as she walked, but neither of them said any more until they were inside the building and Mike had turned on the light.

He looked at her in confusion. She turned out to be a little old lady, looking for all the world like someone's grandmother. She was arranging her black dress and trying to brush away the dampness and the dirt which her method of arrival had imposed on her. Somehow she had managed to hang onto a large black handbag hanging over one arm.

She looked him over and nodded her head as if confirming something to herself. "You look like a nice young man, for all your sudden manners," she said sharply. "Are you one of the young astronauts?"

Mike frowned at her. The fact that he was indeed an astronaut in training was not public knowledge. In fact it was a top secret. Who then was this woman and how had she guessed?

"I think you'd better have a talk with Dr. Van Ness," Mike said. "This is his home you're invading and I'm simply one of his guests." Mike turned toward the door. "And I think you'll be seeing him soon," he added as he heard voices coming from the direction of the main house. Their scuffle had been heard; undoubtedly by now the alarm had been sounded.

In a few more seconds they were joined by several

*Mike looked at her in confusion.*

others. Dr. Van Ness was there, a bathrobe thrown over his pajamas, and at the sight of his bearded features, well known in the world of aviation invention, the little old woman gave a satisfied cluck of approval.

Two guards arrived on the run from the main gate and the house, and shortly after several others, including Johnny Bluehawk's sharp-nosed features, were clustering around the prowler.

Dr. Van Ness looked at the little old woman who was now fumbling about in her handbag. "Haven't I seen you somewhere before?" the scientist asked suddenly, looking at the stranger.

The lady looked up. "Of course you have. I've been at many of your press conferences up in Washington and Langley. I'm Amanda Linnet, correspondent for the Northeast Press Syndicate. Here's my press card." She drew out a blue card and flourished it.

Dr. Van Ness waved it aside. "I remember you now. Yes indeed. What are you doing, trying to sneak in here like this?"

Amanda Linnet tipped her head to one side and peered at him sharply. "I'm after a story of course," she snapped. "I think I've got it, too. This is an astronaut setup, isn't it?"

There was a concerted sucking in of breath from everyone around. Dr. Van Ness stared at her for a moment. "You'd better come up to the main house," he said. "We'll talk this over better there."

Amanda Linnet snapped her purse shut as she returned her press card. "Well," she said, "let's go! I don't have to stand here with all these young bloods gawking around as if they'd never seen a respectable old lady in their lives."

Mike suddenly flushed. "Well, now, ma'am," he said, "you wouldn't be stared at if you had behaved like a lady and knocked at the front door. But you did crawl under the wire, didn't you? And what did you do to the watchdog?"

The gray-haired woman flashed a glance at him and smiled. "You're a nice boy, young fellow, and you're perfectly right. As for the dog, I threw him a meatball with a couple of tranquilizer pills inside it. Made him meek as a lamb. Took the growls out of the hound. So let's go up to the house, and maybe I can wash this dirt off my hands before we settle down to a chat. I'd like some tea anyway."

Mike, feeling bewildered, lifted his eyes and caught the amused stare of his Cheyenne roommate. They both shrugged, and then the group dispersed as the guards returned to their posts and the others to the main house.

Once there, Amanda Linnet did insist on washing, and Johnny went into the kitchen and put on some water for tea and then the little group gathered in

Dr. Van Ness' office. Colonel Drummond came clumping down the stairs in bedroom slippers, stared silently at the stranger, then joined the group.

"Now, Miss Linnet," began Dr. Van Ness, but she interrupted him. "Mrs. Linnet, doctor," she said. "I'm a widow. My husband, Colonel Linnet, died in action during the first World War. He flew with the Lafayette Escadrille in 1916, you know. My son, Captain Linnet, died defending Pearl Harbor in the air."

"Yes, I understand," said Dr. Van Ness patiently, "and you've devoted your life to the cause of aviation ever since. I've read some of your articles and have admired your coverage of air topics. I also know you know just about all the top leaders of aviation, civil and military, by their first names. But this still does not entitle you to trespass here or to attempt to break security laws."

"I'm a reporter," she snapped back, "and I know a story when I can smell it. There's something big going on here—something to do with space flight— and I'm after it. If it's security, I'll acknowledge it when it's proven to me."

Colonel Drummond was getting angry. This amazing old lady, who looked as if she would be more at home on a peaceful bench in St. Petersburg, was acting as if she had a right to know everything. "How'd you learn of the existence of this place and what makes you think it has anything to do with astronautics?" he asked, leaning forward.

"I'll tell you if you'll tell me," she replied calmly. "You know my record. I certainly will do nothing to break secrets, but I want to be in on something. Maybe I know some things you'd like to know."

The colonel and the bearded scientist, two of the three directors of Project Quicksilver (the third was the space-medicine expert Dr. Hugo Holderlin), exchanged quick glances. Drummond nodded. "There may be something valuable you can tell us," he finally said. "I guess we can get you clearance later on, if Washington agrees, to know something in exchange. So suppose you tell us how you got here?"

"Now you're talking sense," said Amanda Linnet. "I was tipped off two months ago to go to the Bahamas and keep a sharp eye open for a Redstone rocket landing. I went there too, made my way down to the telemetry station at Grand Bahama Island, though they wouldn't let me in, and I was out there in a rowboat when I saw what I had come for.

"I saw a parachute come down out of the sky, and attached to it was the kind of space capsule the magazines have told about for the Mercury flights. When it landed in the water, I saw a man in a flying suit come out of it and he was picked up by a boat from the Air Force Missile Testing Range. I had good field glasses. In fact, I'd be inclined to say that maybe the young man who had ridden that rocket and come down on that capsule was this young chap here, the one who was so clever at tackling me."

Mike smiled and felt himself redden. Colonel Drummond glanced at him, said nothing.

Amanda Linnet went on. "Afterwards I asked around, but I couldn't get anyone to admit there had been any Redstone flights with men in the noses. It had to be a secret thing. I checked back at Langley and Washington and I was able to prove that all the seven Mercury astronauts were elsewhere, all present and accounted for. So there just had to be a second space flight project, secretly going on. I snooped around more, went to Canaveral, learned of a couple more Redstone flights after that one, which were also successful I guess as they weren't destroyed to anyone's sight . . ."

Mike glanced at Johnny Bluehawk who had come in with the steaming pot and cups and the tea. Mike knew that Johnny Bluehawk had made a successful flight into outer space a couple of weeks after his own first one. Then Jack Lannigan had also gone up successfully. Jack would be still asleep upstairs, along with the others, Harger, Williams, McMahan, and Stacey.

"It took a good deal of watching and waiting, before I spotted the connection between what I'd seen and your estate here at Skyhook, Dr. Van Ness. But I finally found it. And now suppose you tell me what's going on? When are you going to send one of these young men of yours into orbit?"

Colonel Drummond looked at her. "There's something we haven't learned from you yet. That's how did you first get wind of the Bahama Island area? Who tipped you off? If you can tell us you can be doing a great service to your country, believe me."

Mrs. Linnet's quick blue eyes flicked at him as she sipped her tea. "You know you can't expect a reporter to reveal a source," she said smoothly.

"I think you will," the colonel said, "when you've learned our full story. Your source may be exactly the last clue we need to close the net on a determined and deadly enemy. We'll have to wait until we speak to the National Aeronautics and Space Administration in Washington tomorrow before I can make this clear to you."

"You do that," said the amazing little old lady. "Meanwhile, can you put me up for the night?"

The group broke up shortly after that. When Mike and Johnny went back to their room they sat on their beds and stared at each other. Then they both broke out laughing. There was something so extraordinarily odd in this sweet little old woman turning out to be such an iron-nerved snooper—and an authority on the latest in aviation besides.

"*A reporter can't reveal a source,*" Mrs. Linnet said.

Still, as the colonel had said, maybe this was the breaking point which would guarantee the success of their next step—the circling of the earth by a human being in the first man-carrying satellite.

## CHAPTER 3

TRAITOR'S TRAIL

"SO YOU SEE, Mrs. Linnet," said Colonel Drummond, "throughout the course of Project Quicksilver we have been the target of an attempt to sabotage us or to physically injure our astronauts. But we've not yet been able to arrest the man responsible for these deeds, a man named Tench, nor to find out what his motive is or who is behind him."

The scene was one of the conference rooms on the main floor of the big central building at Skyhook. It was a cozy room, once Dr. Van Ness' private study. Now besides the colonel and Mrs. Linnet, fresh and chipper as a bird in spite of the activities of the night before, there was the bearded Van Ness and Mike Mars himself.

Mike had been asked to join them because he had been the one to capture Tench's agent at Cape Canaveral and also because he had been a special object of Tench's hate.

Amanda Linnet looked at Mike and her eyes twinkled. "Well, now, Mr. Mars," she said, "I know why you were so jumpy last night. With that worry, no wonder you were on the lookout."

Mike smiled and looked embarrassed. "I'm sorry about that," he said, "but I don't really feel worried. I'm sort of confident everything will go all right. And . . . my name isn't really Mars, Mrs. Linnet . . ."

"Call me Grandma," she snapped. "Everybody does. You may as well too."

"O.K. . . . Grandma," Mike laughed softly. "My name is Michael Alfred Robert Samson, and my initials spell out Mars. I always stick my initials on things, and folks sort of call me that. I like it, 'cause it reminds me of my dream of getting to Mars someday—though that's a good many years in the future, I guess." He glanced at Dr. Van Ness then, and everyone smiled.

"And I'm really not a mister. I hold a lieutenant's commission in the Air Force since I finished my training," Mike went on.

"Goodness me," said Grandma Linnet, "that's a lot of correcting, but thank you, son. We reporters do like to get the story straight. If I ever write you up, I want to have it right."

"Uh uh," said Colonel Drummond quickly. "No stories, as I told you before. This is strictly top secret. Washington cleared you this morning; you have an A-1 rating for keeping mum on secrets, and I must ask you to keep absolutely everything you see and hear here under your hat."

The little old lady nodded. "I know. I know. You can trust me. Indeed, I am getting sort of angry about those attempts to hurt our boys. Spy work, do you think?"

Colonel Drummond shook his head. "We are inclined to doubt it. There's something more personal here, something we can't quite get at, but we've no reason to suspect foreign intrigue just yet. Now, can you tell us who tipped you off to go to the Bahamas just at that time and where to look?"

Grandma Linnet frowned. "I think I already have an idea who gave us the tip. Somebody phoned our office when I wasn't in and left a number to call back. I checked on it and called. It was a responsible businessman, I recall, but his name . . . now let me see."

Nobody drew a breath. The room was silent as the three men waited for the amazing little woman to speak. Slowly she nodded. "I have it now," she said, and named a name.

The colonel's face went pale. Mike whistled softly. Dr. Van Ness grunted as if he had been unexpectedly punched in the stomach. They were silent some more. Then the colonel spoke slowly.

"You mustn't say anything further about this, any of you," and he looked at Mike. "Let's not draw any conclusions yet and let's not act as if anyone is under suspicion. I shall notify Air Intelligence, who have been stalled checking back on our troubles, and they will carry the investigation through. Until they can prove the connection, let nothing be said here."

"But, sir," said Mike, "if we have a traitor in our midst, how can we continue with our next step in the space program? Will he not leak it out and endanger the whole thing again?"

Colonel Drummond remained silent awhile, then answered slowly. "Now that we know whom to suspect, I think we can prove our suspicions by deliberately setting a trap. We will go on with our announced program, letting all our astronauts and technicians believe everything is going normally. Meanwhile, we will work out a secret shift in plans that will draw out the mischief maker and let him fall into our hands.

"I think we still have to find Tench and grab him, and the man behind Tench can act as our bait unknowingly. So our program is still officially unchanged."

"What is that program?" Amanda Linnet asked. "Is it the same as the Project Mercury man-in-orbit plan? Are you going to send a man up in an Atlas, put him into orbit as a manned satellite for a few hours, circle the world three times and bring him down again?"

"We are," answered Merlin Van Ness. "Project Quicksilver does not differ from Project Mercury in this regard, except that we are top secret and acting under emergency speed-up orders. We consider our young fliers expendable and they know the added risks and accept them."

"What's more," said Colonel Drummond, "we have already set the date of our first orbital attempt

*"Our first astronaut," Colonel Drummond said.*

40

as a month from now. Our first astronaut, the young man who has had the best record so far, and who has already made two visits to outer space, is going to be this freckle-faced night owl himself, Mike Mars."

Mike turned swiftly and stared at him in surprise. "Gosh," he said, "I didn't know it was going to be me. I thought one of the other fellows deserved the break, because I've already had the luck of being first twice. In fact," he broke off a moment in confusion, "in fact I was even thinking that Rod Harger would have been a fair choice."

"Well," said the colonel, "we had thought of him, but we decided to put our best man first. Time is pressing very hard, for America's big rival in the space race may even now be putting their man into orbit, and we can't afford to lead with a second best, even one who is as good a pilot as Harger. You've been our lucky man twice, if you want to call it luck, and we're going to play you a third time."

Mike sat back, still stunned. He hadn't dared hope to be first in this attempt; it had seemed too much and really the other fellows were quite keen and good. But this was it. In a month—he'd go into orbit. Or perhaps go down to a flaming doom high in the stratosphere—a human meteor plunging down to destruction like Icarus. Satellite of life or meteor of death—which was it to be this time?

## CHAPTER 4

## SHADOW ON THE STARS

The astronauts of the Project Quicksilver were a lively bunch. Though they were hard-studying they were also hard-playing. That afternoon Grandma Linnet saw for herself what no other reporter had ever been allowed to see. There was a basketball game set up that afternoon, after the day's work, and there she watched the fast footwork of seven highly trained and perfectly muscled young fellows.

Jumping center was the redheaded Jack Lannigan, a six-footer who had gained his pilot's wings with the Navy. Jack came from the same part of the country as Mike, who had played opposite him on their respective high school teams and was now jumping center against Jack once again. They had become good friends in spite of or perhaps because of their school rivalry.

Then on Mike's team there was Johnny Bluehawk, who played a fast game, in spite of the Florida heat. He was a Cheyenne from Montana and had made his way up as an Air Force pilot by sheer determination to overcome the obstacles that often confront an Indian boy from a small and poverty-stricken tribe. Mike and Johnny were special pals, had flown together as a team, and were usually inseparable.

Backing up Lannigan was the stocky pale-eyed figure of Rod Harger, Junior. Rod was a first-class pilot, a determined and rugged fighter, whose humorless disposition fitted him to attack and master everything that came his way. Rod did not make friends easily, and it could not be said that any of the other astronauts was his special pal. He confided in none his burning ambition to be the first into space. He played ball with the same deadly precision as he faced his personal ambitions, determined to let nothing stop him.

Hart Williams, a good-looking Air Force pilot, and Joe Stacey, slender and light on his feet, another Navy aviator, were also on Mike's team, while grinning Orin McMahan, Marine pilot, and the seventh of the astronauts backed up Rod and Jack. Orin had fully recovered from the injuries received by the Redstone rocket accident he had been in several weeks ago. Three of the young technicians working on the Skyhook grounds filled in the teams, and the action, in spite of the heat and sun, was fast and furious.

When the game was over, the seven gathered around her laughing and mopping the perspiration

LANNIGAN

WILLIAMS

HARGER

BLUEHAWK

STACEY McMAHAN

from their brows. "How'd we do, Grandma?" asked Lannigan. "You see, Mike may be first in the air, but, by gosh, he can't put a finger on a basketball!"

"Ha!" chortled Mike, "you may have licked us today, but wait. Tomorrow is coming."

The little old woman smiled briefly. "A basketball is one thing, the moon is another. Which of you is going out to put your finger on the moon first?"

Mike shrugged. "Who knows?" he said. "It really doesn't matter. We don't think that way here, ma'am. We like to think that it's the action that counts. We'll all do our duty and cheer each other."

"And you, young man," Grandma Linnet turned to Rod Harger. "How do you feel about it?"

Rod ran a hand through his close-cropped straw colored hair and eyed her. "Mike is right, of course,"

45

he said. "Yet there's no doubt that there'll be a lot in it for the first man to do it. There's fame and fortune there even though we aren't supposed to think of it."

"Well, I don't think of it," said Jack and the others nodded. "So here we are. Waiting for the next step."

They trooped up to their quarters to wash and get ready for chow. Grandma Linnet walked slowly after them studying their retreating backs and sizing them up. That Rod Harger was a cool one, she thought.

Later that evening, after the boys had retired, she and the three directors of Project Quicksilver talked it over again.

"Mike Mars is our best man," said Hugo Holderlin, the German expert on space medicine. "We have checked his records and his body readings during his several flights and he is definitely our first choice. But we don't want him hurt before he takes off. And we don't want him blown up by a faulty rocket."

"This means trapping Tench and his backers before the take-off," said Colonel Drummond. "Yet we must get the Atlas set up and checked off perfectly, without any further waste of time."

"Then how can you do this with Tench still at large?" queried the woman reporter.

"We have worked out a plan," said Van Ness. "It's a little expensive but it should work. We are going ahead with our Atlas, which is being set up at

Cape Canaveral. We are going to put our own astronauts right on the project, have them work right along with the regular pad crew, setting it up, checking it off. This way we hope to beat any sabotage that might be tried by someone not in our project.

"So by having our own fellows right in there they'll be able to keep an eye out and double-check what is going on. As for the problem of one of them being himself involved in the treachery—Harger if he is the one—we will in turn be able to check the work each astronaut is doing. Each one will be responsible for certain features of the assembly."

"It doesn't sound safe to me," said Amanda Linnet. "You're still taking a big risk. There are so many things that can go wrong."

"Exactly," said Colonel Drummond, "and the catch is that we expect them to. I will tell you frankly I shall be disappointed if nothing goes wrong."

"I don't understand," said Grandma Linnet sharply. "How can you make the orbital flight then?"

"You'll see," said the colonel grimly. "As for your part, Mrs. Linnet; at the right time we hope to use you for catching Tench. It will be gradually leaked out that you are the only reporter to be on the inside of a big secret project story. In the right presences—and we think you can guess whose those will be—we want you to drop hints about this flight. It is

47

our belief that you will be contacted by Tench or by his backer. He will want to use you as a tool. Your duty is to appear to be willing to consider such illegal assistance in getting a big news scoop."

"In short, I'm going to be the bait in the trap, eh?" Amanda Linnet allowed a thin smile to cross her face. Her eyes twinkled. "I think I like that idea. Yessir, I think it'll give me a pleasure to lead the rats to the trap."

"Now, hold on," said Merlin Van Ness. "We don't expect you to get into any danger. Don't get any ideas of collaring them yourself. Let us and the Air Intelligence do the actual grabbing."

"Hmm. I can at least get one swat with my umbrella on their heads, can't I?" the little lady retorted, and then burst into laughter. "Great heavens, can you see me doing it, though!"

They all laughed and relaxed.

Upstairs Mike Mars put down the book he was reading and switched off the light. Johnny Bluehawk was already asleep. He heard the faint sounds of laughter reach him from downstairs and smiled to himself. The stars were waiting for him. The orbit was waiting. He could see himself now, riding through space, circling the world, a human satellite, and the picture was good. But as he fell asleep, it seemed to him that his mental picture of himself as a human moon was being obscured. There was a shadow crossing the face of the moon Mike, and it was like an eclipse. He frowned in his sleep at the image. Eclipsed . . . and the shadow that blocked his path through the stars was that of another man, another person, short and stocky, but somehow, because he was now asleep, he couldn't quite recall whose shadow it was.

CHAPTER 5

## WIRE BY WIRE, BOLT BY BOLT

THE Atlas, designed and manufactured by Convair, is America's first truly operational intercontinental ballistic missile. It has proven to be the most reliable high-power rocket in the hands of the free world. What made it so valuable to space research is that it is the first liquid fuel rocket that could boost itself into orbit without extra rocket stages.

Working on the Atlas, the astronauts realized just how clever a missile it was. When the older idea of riding one rocket on top of another, firing off the second stage at the moment the first dropped off, and thereby gaining additional power, was finally attempted, the complications became very serious. There were too many gadgets to work with, too many little things to go wrong with that piggyback system of space flight.

The Atlas, which first was tested in 1957, managed to avoid the problem of being a two or three stage rocket by a new system. Its engineers called it a one-and-a-half stage rocket—and so it was.

It does have booster engines, a sustainer engine, and guidance engines. But instead of each being mounted to its own fuel tanks, perched one on top of the other, and being dependent on some tiny electric connection to set each off at the right time after the main booster had lifted the entire mass, all these engines are connected to the same system of tanks.

The Atlas is thus one fuel tank storage system to which all three types of rockets are attached. At the moment of firing all the major rocket tubes blast together. The boosters and the sustainer together work to raise the rocket. At the right time, the booster engines shut down and drop off along with their equipment. The main fuel tank now supplies liquid oxygen and fuel to the sustainer engine alone. There is no hitch in the propulsion of the rocket, for this sustainer, located in the center of the driving end of the Atlas, has been firing all along. It goes on, driving the Atlas ever faster and higher until at the time of its burn-out, it has achieved the desired orbital speed. There is still fuel for the two small "vernier" rockets which then come into play to guide the Atlas into the desired direction, to correct any inaccuracy of motion or orbit.

The result of this single-fuel-tank system, eliminating the terrible complexities of the several stage mis-

sile has been the most successful series of flights the United States has achieved. Most of the space satellites we have launched, and our interplanetary probes as well, have been Atlas riders.

That is why, as Colonel Drummond explained to the astronauts, the Atlas was chosen to carry the first man into space. It could be relied upon to lift the load of the space capsule, with its human pilot inside, into space, then to place it in orbit around the Earth, fast enough to circle the Earth like a moon, yet slow enough not to send it off into outer space to escape forever.

Mike Mars understood this very well, yet he was thrilled and excited by the Atlas they were working on now. The thing had been perfected—as nearly as anything using the highly tricky liquid fuels and liquid gases could be called perfect—and yet it was so new that no one could be entirely sure of it. It had been as late as 1959 that it had been finally pronounced "operational" by the Air Force.

"One secret of missile work," said the colonel as they arrived at Complex 34, "is endless testing. Nothing must be overlooked. Everything must be checked and double-checked. So get ready for a full schedule."

They scattered to their tasks, each man joining the allotted team of Atlas missilemen, working with them. The missile standing now on its pad—it was mighty big when you stood at its base, towering like a seven-story house—was weighed empty and its weight when loaded estimated. Cables were fitted to it on special sockets that would supply its internal power systems from outside. Not until the moment of launching would the rocket use its own power sources; until then power came from outside, through those cables, which were checked and registered from within the big domelike blockhouse.

Inside the blockhouse panels of consoles and gauges registered everything that went on inside the Atlas. Line by line each system was tried, checked, and tried again. The fuel tanks and valves were tested, first empty, then partly filled, emptied again, and once more.

Wire by wire, tube by tube, valve by valve, pipe by pipe, and bolt by bolt, the entire complex missile was gone over. The hydraulics system—was it in order? Test it, check it, worry about it. What about the pneumatics, the air pumps systems? Test them. Worry about them.

The telemetry system—the means by which those on the ground would know whether the Atlas was working right, the only means by which they would get valuable answers to the questions the rocket has been designed to answer—that was important. Check it out, trace it down.

The flight control? Is that in order? And the propulsion system—is that operating slick and clean? Last but not least, what of the launcher release? If that fluffed, the whole thing could go in ruins.

Mike worked at the capsule, which was one of several now on hand in the special astronautics hangar. When he was confident it was in complete order—he had to check every part of its electrical and pumping systems just as carefully as the rocket that would launch it was checked—he rode with it to the Atlas.

He was there when the workmen lifted it up to the top of the silver Atlas, was on the job when it was attached to the nose cone of the launching missile. With the capsule on, the Atlas was even higher—with another twenty feet added to it—though part of that was just the frame of the capsule's towering emergency rocket escape system.

The capsule looked set and solid at last. A week had gone by. Mike came down slowly from that final examination, riding down in the gantry elevator. He met Johnny Bluehawk at the ground level wiping his hands on a cloth, clearing them of grease. Jack Lannigan came up from around the engine to join them.

"Looks good, Mike," said Johnny. "We're ready for the rehearsal loading and the first static test firing. Tomorrow morning."

"Yep," said Jack, "it's going to be a full-dress rehearsal, complete countdown and all. If all is well, we can count on getting you off in another week."

The three walked down the ramp in silence. Johnny commented slowly, "You know, I wish I had the faith Dr. Van Ness has in all of us astronauts. If one of us is a saboteur he sure handed him a royal chance to do you dirt. With all of us working right on this missile, the chance of jamming the works is good."

"Who do you mean?" asked Jack curiously. "You think one of us was behind the sabotage? You never said that before."

"Johnny has had this idea for some time," said Mike quietly. "At first I didn't believe him either, but I've come to think he's right. I think the reason we're all working on this flight ourselves is to find out who would be responsible for whatever does go wrong."

Jack whistled. "That makes you the guinea pig, Mike," he said. "I hope you trust me, by gosh."

Mike laughed. "Right now, I intend to trust everybody. Keep mum about this, will you?"

Jack nodded. Johnny grunted. "I don't like it, just the same."

"We'll find out if anything is O.K. in the test run. That should prove everything," said Mike.

"And what's to stop him from bollixing things up at the last moment, next week?" retorted his Cheyenne friend.

Mike didn't answer.

## CHAPTER 6

## THE VOICE OF TROUBLE

THERE was something eerie about the rehearsal countdown. The scene was exactly the same as if the big shoot was under way. Men sat hunched in the closed blockhouse, behind walls fifteen feet thick, while a voice droned out the minutes and seconds. Point by point the checking proceeded.

Clustered in a group in the rear of the blockhouse, where they would not interfere with the men at the instrument panels, the seven astronauts observed every instant of the long count. It took over three hours to recheck every wire and gauge in the mighty rocket outside.

Meanwhile, as they could see by observing the four television screens which gave a four-sided view of the gleaming silvery rocket, the Atlas had been fueled, and wisps of white vapor were coiling and writhing about its base, while a white hoar-frost coated its silvery sides.

There was a difference, of course. At the strategic

moment, when the mighty red-and-white painted gantry would have been rolled away on its tracks, and the rocket left ready to rise into the skies, the great metal framework remained, its clamps tightly holding to the missile. It would not fly this day. This was just a test.

But somehow it was serious, so real, that the fellows almost expected it to go. As the countdown got to ten minutes, to three, then to seconds, they found themselves almost holding their breaths. Even the missilemen in the blockhouse caught the moment. Though many of these men had attended the flight of other Atlases, had been present at the historic moments when weather satellites and planet probes had gone up, they too hunched silently over the panels, watching the glowing lights that indicated the life inside the rocket.

At the zero point, there was a brief flash of fire. The rocket was fired, for a moment, for a split second, then cut off. The steam rose high, as the waters poured on the base of the pad to cool and counter the powerful jet. Then the test was over. The rocket was emptied of its remaining fuels, the results of the countdown were carefully gathered together and checked for study the next day.

"Everything seems in perfect order," said Mike to Johnny Bluehawk. "Not a hitch this time."

"That's right," said the Cheyenne, "but there are

still things that can happen between now and the real firing. How long is that going to be?"

Rod Harger, standing near them, looked up briefly, his icy pale eyes resting on Mike's smiling freckled features, then on Johnny's dark hook-nosed ones.

"The date I heard is five days from now," said Rod. "There's a day's rest for us tomorrow, and then back on the job. By this time next week the first American will have been in orbit."

Mike nodded thoughtfully, glanced at Rod. "The capsule's ready, that's for sure," he said. Rod looked back at him, their eyes locking for a moment. Then Rod quickly turned away.

They returned to Skyhook early in the afternoon and found time for rest. The next day was a Sunday. The astronauts would do as they pleased that day, go into town, take a plane if they could find one available at the Orlando bases, in short take it easy.

Rod Harger went into Orlando with two of the other astronauts. He left the others in the town with an excuse and went on until he was sure no one had followed him. He found a phone in a public booth, called a number.

Up North in a wealthy suburb of a great city, a man strangely like Rod Harger answered the phone. He was as stocky as Rod, his hair was of the same pale yellow color, though streaked with gray, his eyes were hard and cold, though wrinkled with the hard lines of years of ruthless drive. "Hello, son," he said, and his son, the young astronaut, answered in the same quick sharp tone.

"Dad," said Rod, "the date is set. Thursday. If something doesn't stop him, Mike Mars will go up that day and be the first man in space. Have you made any plans this time that won't go haywire?"

"Don't get sarcastic with me, son," said his father. "I've told you what's in this for us and I never go back on my plans. Are you getting cold feet? Want to let Mike go ahead and cop the credit that you could get?"

Rod in the phone booth bit his lip. "I've gone through this far. I've done all the dirty things you've set up for me. Frankly, it hasn't helped. We haven't put me first yet."

The senior Harger scowled. "According to what you told me, if Mike doesn't go, you will go up. Is that right?"

When Rod agreed that this was so, his father continued. "We tried sabotaging the Redstones before—and you say you've the opportunity to do it now. I don't trust that. It's too easy. As you explained it to me they could trace any sabotage this time to the astronaut responsible.

"So don't sabotage this Atlas, not yet anyway. There is a different approach. We've got to get Mike Mars! Get rid of him, and the coast is clear."

Rod hesitated a moment. "How do we get rid of him?"

"This time Tench and I will see that the job is done. You stay out of it, except as a last resort. Mike Mars must die! I'll see that you get something to take care of him at the last minute if we fail—but we won't fail this time." Rod Harger, Senior, was snarling.

"What do I do?" asked Rod softly.

"You stand pat. Keep working. Hang around. When the time for the flight comes, get ready to take Mike's place, because he isn't going to be there! Tench will see you later today—he's still in Florida —and he'll give you something to hold against emergencies. Can you stay in town a few more hours?"

When Rod agreed, he got some instructions and then hung up. He wasted time around Orlando until that evening. At the right time, he was standing on a quiet crossroads in a nearly deserted section at the edge of town. A car came along, slowed to a halt. Rod ran over to it.

A man reached out over the steering wheel, a man Rod did not recognize until he saw the barely concealed tiny hooked scar on his cheek. This man, the renegade ex-flier Tench who had made so much

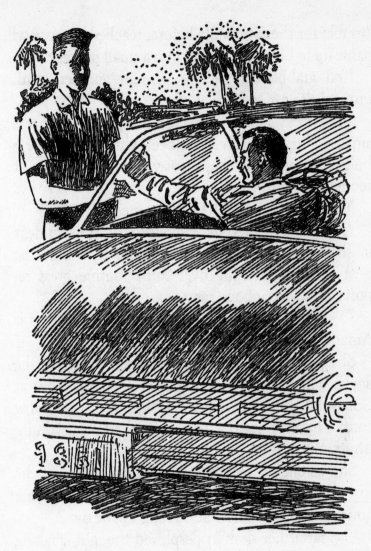

*The man handed Rod a package.*

trouble for the astronauts before, reached out as Rod came up to him and handed him a small package.

Rod grabbed it; Tench, without another word, gunned the car and drove off.

The stocky Harger pocketed the package—it was small enough to fit in his pocket without much of a bulge—turned and went away from the place of rendezvous with equal speed.

Mike Mars must die! That was the keyword.

A little gray-haired old lady was sitting at her desk in the offices of the Northeast Press Syndicate the next morning, looking over some routine press reports, when her phone rang.

"Yes," she snapped, as she picked it up. "This is Amanda Linnet. Who's calling?"

She listened in silence a moment. "You say the day is Thursday, eh? I should be on the lookout at Canaveral this Thursday for a big news break. How come I haven't heard a word from the Space Administration people about this?"

She listened a moment. "You aren't talking, eh? Just who is this? Hello! Hello?" She put the phone down, mumbled to herself, "Hung up, he did."

She sat at her desk in perplexed thought, shaking her head. "Something's not working out the way we thought," she said to herself. "Something's haywire with our trap." She picked up her phone, dialed long distance. When the call came through, she began, "Hello, Merlin, something's cooking we hadn't quite counted on. I can't figure it, yet. Listen to this. I just got a call . . ."

## CHAPTER 7

## ON YOUR MARK, GET SET!

"THIS is the big week," said Merlin Van Ness, standing before the blackboard in the study room at Skyhook. "I want to go over once more just briefly the nature of our plan."

The seven young astronauts sat tensely in their seats, facing the board and their bearded science director. With the moment of action just a few days away, with the rocket ready and waiting, checked out, tight and final, things were different.

The sun seemed brighter, the sky seemed bluer, the day just a bit sharper to their senses. It was as if they were coming alive as they never had before. To Mike Mars, tense in his seat, it reminded him of that day when he was first called upon to solo his plane—when his long hours of study and student-flying were to be tested alone in the air, when his own life was in his hands, trusted to his newly learned skills.

"The capsule containing the astronaut will be lifted into space by the booster power of the Atlas rocket. It will be launched from Cape Canaveral over the Atlantic Ocean in a direction a little north of due east. The astronaut during this time will be under pressure inside the capsule and he will be expected to do nothing save try to retain consciousness, and be ready to utilize the safety ejection mechanism if the need should arise during this stage of the flight.

"The capsule will achieve orbital velocity between one hundred and one hundred and fifty miles up at which time it will be traveling at about eighteen thousand miles an hour. When it achieves this planned point of speed and altitude, it will be sepa-

rated from the Atlas booster missle by its own small separation rocket motors."

Dr. Van Ness drew a diagram on the board to show the rising of the rocket and the point of separation. He continued:

"Now the capsule will rise with the astronaut lying down in his contour chair, his back aligned with the base of the capsule, which contains the heat shield. At the time of separation, on achieving orbit, the capsule will turn a half somersault, shifting its position one hundred and eighty degrees until the wide end, the heat shield is facing forwards. At this time the astronaut will then be actually flying backwards through space.

"As you know this shift is necessary when the time for return to the atmosphere comes. For then the heat shield will serve to protect the capsule from the extremes of temperature that will be encountered during the re-entry into the air belt of the Earth. Also it will again place the capsule in the best position for the use of its parachutes and other slowdown mechanisms."

The bearded director's chalk quickly sketched the capsule turning over.

"The capsule will be in orbit, in free fall about the Earth. It will be allowed to make three circuits of the Earth. That is to say, if nothing goes wrong, if the astronaut reports no problems. If there are grounds for concern, we can bring the capsule down after the first orbit.

"At all times we will be in telemetric communication with the capsule, we will know what is going on within it. We will be in radio communication with the astronaut and he will be expected to maintain ground contact. There is a belt of tracking stations around the world and at all times he should be within the range of at least one of them. The control of the capsule will be automatic, and if everything is working right, it will perform as directed from the ground. However, the astronaut is able to take control of it at any time, and can assume control should he find it necessary.

"When the time for re-entry arrives, the retro-rockets will be fired. This will be at a point in the orbit between Hawaii and the western coast of the United States. These rockets will be sufficient to slow the capsule enough to bring it out of orbital velocity and to start it down toward the surface of the Earth. At about the time it will be over Florida, these rockets will be dropping and the capsule will begin to feel the drag of the atmosphere. This drag will slow it down steadily, until such a time as its parachute system can be brought into play and the capsule finally brought down to the surface of the sea. The capsule will then land on the ocean in the area of the Atlantic Missile Range."

He put the chalk down, looked at the seven young men. Mike Mars sat back, looked to his right at Johnny Bluehawk. The Indian seemed lost in thought, as if studying in his mind the flight of this tiny metal box with its human inhabitant.

Mike looked to his left at Rod Harger. Strangely, Rod seemed rather happy. He had a half-smile on his face and he too seemed lost in thought, as if following in his mind's eye the rise and landing of a space hero.

The gray-eyed astronaut ran a hand through his stubborn shock of sandy hair, and wondered what Rod was planning. He knew something that the other astronauts had not been told of, but he wondered now whether Rod had something in plan that nobody had anticipated.

"Now, gentlemen," said Van Ness, "let us be on our way."

Johnny Bluehawk raised a hand then. When Van Ness nodded to him, Johnny asked quietly, "We all know that Mike Mars has been picked to be the first astronaut to attempt this flight. Will he ride this rocket on Thursday?"

Van Ness looked at Johnny sharply. "Such are our plans," he said slowly.

"And if Mike, for some reason, cannot make it,

is sick perhaps, will the flight be postponed?" continued Johnny.

Dr. Van Ness hesitated. "We have made preparations for this shoot—and others to follow—and we will go through on schedule. You have all been made aware of the list of preference. If one man cannot be ready, the next man will go. But only when it is absolutely certain that the substitution is necessary. To judge from Mike Mars' healthy looks, unless he gets a bad case of sunburn, he will be there."

Johnny did not smile. Mike looked wonderingly at his old friend. What was on Johnny's mind? he thought.

Rod Harger also looked over at Johnny Bluehawk. Was this redskin getting ideas? he said to himself. If Mike doesn't go up, I will be the next in line, not this fellow. And, this I know—on Thursday, I will be in the capsule, not Mike.

They went on then by bus and plane over to the great space field and the Atlas on Complex 34. They passed, as they had passed day after day, the distant towers of the other rocket pads, row after row, the gantries and blockhouses that fitted the Titans and the Thors, the Minutemen, and the Redstones. There were several other Atlas installations, and on two or three the forms of other Atlas rockets standing gleaming upright could be made out in the distance.

71

There was always activity at Canaveral. Were any of those other Atlas missiles ready for flight? Were any to be given to them after this first flight?

One of the astronauts had asked questions like that but he had gotten no answers. Nobody knows all that is going on at Canaveral. There is too much and it is better not to know all of the secrets. That way, there is the delight of the unexpected.

Tuesday found Mike on the top level of the high framework working on the capsule attachments, checking out the wiring, and chatting with the two missilemen who were working with him. He paused a moment and looked out across the fields.

Below him hung the dozen or so stories of the metal framework, and he could see the helmeted figures of the ground men like ants walking about on the cement ramp and clustered about the motors at the base. He could see the bump of the blockhouse with two or three figures standing outside. He could see the little inspection post and he could see the road leading from this particular complex. He also could see a tiny blue staff car making its way up that road and stopping at the guard post.

Mike watched and he saw two tiny figures emerge from the car, talk to someone, then start off towards the gantry. One he recognized as Colonel Drummond from his gray hair and his stride. The other . . . well, it was a woman or a girl, he wasn't sure.

*Mike saw two figures head for the gantry.*

A tiny figure, Mike thought, could it be Vivian Van Ness? No, this one had gray hair. Why, he thought, it must be Grandma Linnet.

Now, what could be bringing her here? Mike put his hands on his hips and looked down. They were coming up to the capsule on the top of the Atlas, he was sure. Did this mean something was up?

In a few minutes the open frame elevator rattled up its shaft and the colonel and the little old lady popped out.

"How's it going, young man?" Amanda Linnet asked.

Mike touched his white-painted workman's helmet respectfully. "Very well, ma'am," he said. "How'd you happen to come down today?"

"Well, now, Mike," she said, her eyes twinkling, "a little bird told me something was going to happen this week."

"That's not far wrong," said the colonel. "Some little bird has been chirping too much around here. Several other reporters have been turning up in the Cocoa Beach motels yesterday and today. I'm beginning to wonder if we were figuring our enemy's plans quite right."

Mike stared over their heads and out across the array of mighty rocket installations. He felt confident. "It seems so petty," he said slowly, "to let

74

personal attitudes get in the way of something so vast and big for all people."

"People are people," said Grandma Linnet, "and by the time you get to my age, you learn to expect just about anything. Oh," she paused, reaching into her bag, "this telegram just came for you. I picked it up at Skyhook when I went to join the colonel there and the clerk asked me to bring it along."

Mike took the yellow envelope, looked at it a moment. Now who could be sending him urgent messages? He slit it open with a finger, unwrapped the message, and read it swiftly. He gasped.

## CHAPTER 8

## FOUR GO NORTH

"WHAT is it?" asked Colonel Drummond when he saw how upset Mike had become.

The young astronaut handed the slip of paper to him. The colonel glanced at it, and Grandma Linnet stood up on her toes and looked over his shoulder at the message.

It read simply, *Your mother is very ill, calling for you. Please return home at once. Signed, Father.*

Mike was pale. "Colonel," he said. "I know the flight is coming due, but would it be possible for me to be given leave at once?"

The colonel still held the telegram in his hand, staring at it, and Grandma Linnet was still beside him, looking off into the distance as if also buried in thought. Suddenly she smiled, then as if afraid Mike might have noticed it, she suppressed it. She tapped the colonel on the arm.

He looked up at her, ignoring Mike's question for the moment. She looked the colonel in the eye, and with her back slightly turned away from Mike, she winked and nodded.

Drummond exhaled slowly, then looked at Mike. "All right," he said. "I think you can make it. Your work here is just rechecking what we are already sure is in order. Besides, you already know the special secret of this flight. I think you can get home to see your mother."

They went down together to the base of the pad, returned to the blockhouse. There the colonel made some phone calls. Hanging up, he went to Mike standing just outside the door with Mrs. Linnet.

"I'm sorry that I can't seem to arrange any immediate transport from the Air Force bases nearby. They don't have a thing going to Ohio today, and I can't commandeer any spare jets on their fields. I've called the airport at Miami however, and booked you passage north on a regular airliner. You've just got time to get down to Patrick Air Base here and they do have a flight that will take you to Miami in time to catch your plane to Columbus. From there you can arrange transportation to your home town."

"Good," said Mike, "and thank you, sir. I'll catch the same car you just arrived in and get on to the base now. I'll phone you from home when I can."

"Keep cool, Mike," said the colonel, "and— there's one thing more."

Mike, about to dash for the waiting car, turned.

The colonel went inside the blockhouse for a moment and then returned carrying a leather belt and a holstered Army pistol. "I want you to put this on and wear it at all times. Remember my orders about self-protection."

Mike took the holster and belt, but seemed confused. "But, sir, at home . . ." The colonel shook his head, became very crisp. "This is an order, Lieutenant Samson," he said very firmly. "You are to wear side arms at all times when you are away from here."

Mike was surprised at his tone, but snapping a salute, he ran once more for the car, while buckling the heavy military automatic about his waist.

No sooner had the blue car driven off than the colonel turned swiftly around, and grasped Amanda Linnet by the arm. "Amanda," he said in a low voice, "is this it?"

"I'm sure," she snapped back. "In fact I know it is. This is the trap that's waiting for Mike. Because his mother is not sick. At least she wasn't three days ago when I paid her a visit myself. I was checking up on Mike's past, for the news story that I'm going to write some day when it's finally public knowledge.

"Mike's mother is in great health, and I certainly don't believe she took sick overnight. This telegram is a trick."

The colonel nodded, his weathered narrow eyes gleaming. "Then we're ready for action too." He went back to the phone and put in another series of calls.

While he was calling, Amanda Linnet on his instructions rounded up Johnny Bluehawk and Jack Lannigan. These two came up, removing the white crash helmets they had been wearing around the gantry.

"I've got a special mission for you two," the colonel snapped. "We're heading back for McCoy Air Base at Orlando right away. Don't say anything to the other fellows. Dr. Van Ness will explain it to them later."

Mike Mars would have been perplexed if he had been able to follow the progress of his commander and friends in the next few hours. For they speeded away from Canaveral, away from the direction that Mike was heading in. In an hour they were at the central Florida airbase, where they rushed out of their car, ran to the operations building. Shortly afterwards the three Quicksilver men emerged clad in flying outfits, and walked to two silvery jets being tuned up on the field.

It was not long before the two jets took off, one flown by Johnny Bluehawk and carrying the colonel as passenger, and the other flown singly by Jack Lannigan. The two supersonic interceptors rose on roaring smoke streams, and soon vanished northwards into the high blue Florida sky.

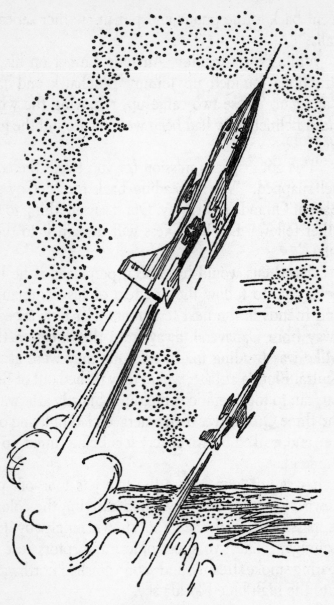

*The two jets soon vanished northwards.*

Mike thought about his mother all during his ride to Patrick Air Force Base. Though this base was but fifteen miles down the long strip of beach which was the resort village of Cocoa Beach, it seemed to Mike that it was a long and tiresome trip. He was anxious to get going. It seemed a shame the colonel couldn't have arranged for him to borrow a fast jet. He could have been home in Ohio in a couple of hours. This way it seemed likely to take a half day at least.

When Mike got to Patrick he was upset to find another delay facing him. The courier plane which was to leave for Miami International Airport was not quite ready and Mike had to wait around almost an hour before it took off. He sat and thought.

His mother had been in good health when last he had seen her, a visit he had made a month ago. Her letters had indicated no illness. Just what did she come down with that was so sudden and so serious? He knew his father would not have been so emphatic if it wasn't a matter of life and death.

Mike had always been interested in planes and flying and his mother had had to steel herself against worrying about the risks involved in his career as an Air Force jet pilot. Though, as a matter of maintaining secrecy, she did not know what project he was with nor exactly what he was doing. As a matter of fact, it occurred to Mike, his mother did not know the address of Skyhook, but had assumed he was based at McCoy.

He fished the telegram from his pocket and glanced at the address. It was sent directly to Skyhook. That was odd, Mike thought. Could he have accidentally mentioned this address last time he was home? He was sure he wouldn't, for Mike was not a blabbermouth and not likely to make slips.

It was strange, though. How had his father known he was at Skyhook? For that matter, how had he even heard of the place?

Well, no matter, the plane was warming up now.

At Miami, the jinx of delay still seemed to be haunting him. The plane the colonel had said would be ready, was already loaded and Mike couldn't get passage. The next plane was two hours later, and Mike finally had to board that one, with noontime come and gone.

The flight, at civilian air line speeds, seemed endless to Mike, though the passengers, returning from vacationing on the Florida sands, marveled at its speed. It was late in the afternoon when Mike put down at Columbus.

Arranging a private plane to fly him to his home town, in the middle of the state, took more time, and when at last the little propeller-driven plane landed, the sun was setting and twilight was on the scene.

Mike breathed the air of his native state and felt

again the nostalgia of his childhood. This air, with its scent of farmland and hay and harvest, was good. He felt like a boy again, and only the thought of his mother hanging between life and death in her room at home in the town that spread out before him, made him feel unhappy and uneasy.

His bad luck continued to haunt him. He couldn't get a taxi. He finally was able to wave down a passing car, coming from the day's work, and got a hitch to the street where his house stood.

In the darkening evening, Mike said good-by to the kind driver, and started off toward his home, near the farther end of the street.

He walked fast, striding quickly, wondering what he would find. He was in his Air Force blues, a short Eisenhower jacket his protection against the autumn air, the annoying weight of his revolver thumping against his side. He carried no baggage, for he'd no time for that.

He did not notice a large black car parked at the side of the road by a large shade tree, whose shadow now darkened a patch of the sidewalk. Nor did he notice another large car, standing silently at the distant corner of the street.

As he came into the shadow of the tree, passing the first and nearer car, he did not see that there was a man standing in the shadow, and not until the man stepped up quickly behind him, grabbed Mike by the shoulder, and clamped a hand over his startled face, did Mike realize he was not alone.

He struggled to break free, but the strangling hand bent him back with the advantage of the surprise attack and another figure popped from the car and joined the assault.

Mike kicked but found himself lifted off his feet, his hands held tight, and something struck him hard. He was dazed and felt himself being swiftly dragged into the parked car. As he was shoved onto the floor of the rear seat and the two attackers leaped in to hold him down and slam the door, another person, in the front, stepped on the accelerator. The car shot forward and sped off down the street.

As it passed the end of the street and turned, the second car came to life. It too started to move and then, a half block behind the first car, it followed along, with its lights out.

*Something struck him hard.*

## CHAPTER 9

## KILLER COUNTDOWN

Mike fumbled groggily for his automatic, but the rough hands of his captors swiftly reached down and withdrew it before he could grasp it. Desperately Mike tried to raise himself from the floor of the car, but the surprise with which he had been attacked had left him breathless and his head still rang from the unfair blow that had been struck him.

The two men holding him managed to tie his hands with a piece of rope and one of them shoved a handkerchief into Mike's mouth to keep him from crying out. Then the larger of them simply sat on the young astronaut to hold him still while the car continued to drive swiftly and silently through the streets.

It came to a halt somewhere outside the town. Mike was dragged to his feet and pushed from the car. It was now nearly dark outside but he could make out trees and countryside and a dark building alongside a rural road, like an abandoned farmhouse.

Into this place the two men pushed him, while the third drove the car around the building and out of sight from the road.

Inside, the place was dark but a flick of a switch revealed to Mike's eyes that he was in the living room of a badly run-down and poorly furnished home. It smelled as if it had been deserted for many months; there was the musty odor of a closed house and he could feel the dampness of slow decay.

They shoved him to a seat on a crumbling old couch, whose bare springs projected in spots through the worn and shabby covering. The light from a bare bulb inserted in a fixture hanging from the ceiling allowed him the first good look at his captors.

One he did not recognize—a shifty looking individual with the kind of red nose that betrayed the habitual drunkard. This one, Mike reasoned correctly, was probably some common thug hired for the occasion.

He knew the other man, though. It was Tench.

Tench, who had once gone under the assumed name of Cahoon, was looking down on Mike with an ugly grin on his face. He was gaunt, and the tiny hooked scar on his cheek showed up red from the efforts of his tussle with Mike. Tench, Mike knew, had once been a pilot in the Air Force, but he had been dishonorably discharged for good cause and had thereafter borne a grudge against the service and his country. Tench was the chief agent of the series of efforts to block or sabotage Project Quicksilver.

"Take a good look," sneered Tench now as he saw Mike eyeing him. "You may not have long to do so."

"You won't get away with this," said Mike defiantly. "Whatever your game is, you can't stop the astronauts."

"Oh, I'm not trying to stop the astronauts—or one of them anyway. I'm just going to stop you—haven't you figured that out yet? We want the astronaut project to succeed—with the right man."

At this moment the man who had been driving the car came in, shutting the door behind him. Mike looked at him and was instantly struck by a strange feeling of familiarity. He realized he had never seen this man before, but the stocky figure, the pale, washed-out eyes, the short pale hair now graying which still showed signs of the faded straw it had once been, resembled someone he knew.

In a second it came to him that he was looking at a man who could be none other than Rodney S. Harger, Senior, father of his fellow astronaut.

Mike stared at him in silence. Now he realized the secret behind all the long series of attacks that had been made on himself and his friends. The older Harger glanced briefly at Mike, then nodded to Tench and the two of them went to a corner of the room and began whispering together.

Mike remembered the suspicions that his friend Johnny Bluehawk had several times tried to communicate to him. In all those times Mike had refused to accept the Cheyenne's personal conviction that Rod Harger was out to harm him. But here, in the person of Rod's father, was the evidence.

At the same time Mike realized a more ominous thought. Never, now that he had actually seen the man who had been behind Tench's work, would he be allowed to return to reveal his knowledge. These men meant to kill him. It was the only way they could keep their secret.

And it would gain them their objective—if that objective was to have Rod Harger the first man in space!

For what else could have been their objective? Mike knew that that was the answer.

He looked at the two talking in the corner, and without hearing them knew that they were discussing murder. He looked at the seedy thug watching him from a broken-down chair against the wall, and wondered whether he should attempt to make an escape.

Mike's hands were tied in front of him but with the thug's eyes on him, he couldn't hope to break loose. The sandy-haired astronaut faked a groan, then fell back on the couch and rolled over on his stomach, facing the wall.

As he had hoped, his captors thought Mike merely

sick and suffering. They paid no attention to him. He saw one of the broken springs projecting from the edge of the couch near the wall, and working his hands over it, sawed carefully away across the rough loose end of the spring. It would be slow, but he might be able to make the ropes frayed enough to break apart.

He worked carefully, and for a few minutes was not interrupted. But then he heard the footsteps of the two others come up to him, felt a hand roughly grab him, turn him over.

"Time to get up, Mars," said Tench. "You're going for one last ride now. Better start saying your prayers, because you're heading for the stars now—one way by spirit express!"

Mike struggled to his feet, trying hard to look weaker than he felt. Mike had always prided himself on keeping his body in good condition and the truth was that he had thrown off the pain of his attackers' blow. He was tense, his blood surging and ready for a supreme effort to escape.

As he rose to his feet, Tench stepped back and leveled Mike's own automatic. "Keep your distance, and start toward the door," commanded the renegade.

Mike started toward the door, doing his best to stumble and weave about. He glanced back.

Rod Harger, Senior, was standing away from

Tench, watching with fascination. The thug was also standing away from the doorway. Tench was holding the heavy military pistol on Mike, apparently waiting for him to reach the doorway. In a flash Mike knew that when he touched that door, Tench would fire.

Mike rushed forward and just as he reached the door Tench raised the gun. Suddenly Mike dropped to the floor, rolled swiftly over, and grabbed for the legs of the old chair the thug had vacated.

Tench fired. The explosion of the automatic was deafening in the closed room, and the bullet crashed into the floor just over Mike's head.

Frantically Mike's hands swept against the leg of the chair and he shoved it across in Tench's direction. The big thug aimed once more, fired once again, while jumping out of the way of the chair. The bullet crashed into the wall a few inches above Mike's ear.

As Mike struggled to roll out of the way, he saw Tench pause, take careful aim. His mind told him at once that this time there'd be no escape.

He heard the thug and Harger yelling, but all he could see was Tench's face, grinning like a demon, and the gun leveling at him.

There was another shot from somewhere, but it was not from Tench's gun. Instead the murderer's face changed expression as if amazed. His gun fell to the floor, and a spout of blood covered his gun hand.

Mike leaped to his feet, ripping free of the ropes

*The bullet hit the door over Mike's head.*

and as he did so someone came through the broken window. The someone, wearing Air Force blue, with a smoking gun in his hand, fired a shot at Tench who had turned and was trying to get at his own pistol in his pocket.

Tench staggered, whirled around.

The newcomer, black-haired, curved nosed, ruddy of skin, turned his pistol on the two other criminals in the room. "Stand where you are!" shouted Johnny Bluehawk. "Don't move an inch!"

In terror the elder Harger and the shaking thug raised their hands.

Jack Lannigan poked his head through the window next, waving his own service automatic. "All clear?" he asked. "Who's got the ball?"

"I've got the ball," sang out Mike, swooping down and rescuing his own gun from the floor where Tench had let it drop. "This is my basket now."

Jack climbed in, went to the door, opened it. "Come on in," he said. "Make yourself at home."

Colonel Drummond came in, looking swiftly around. "Good work, boys," he said. "Good astronautic timing. The countdown was perfect."

Mike Mars looked at the colonel and suddenly chuckled. "Were you men around this long? How'd you find me anyway. Say . . . what's this countdown anyway? Don't tell me you were expecting this?"

Johnny Bluehawk laughed. "You were the bait,

Mike. This time we set a trap for them and they fell in. I think we've caught the big fish this time." He glanced at the elder Harger, still white-faced.

The colonel looked at Harger too. "Yes, I think we can see the motive now behind all this dirty work."

"My boy had nothing to do with this," said the elder Harger suddenly. "He knows nothing about all this. Nothing at all. It was all my doing."

The colonel glanced once more around the room, then fixed Harger with his own eyes, eyes weathered from the sun of a hundred flights, from looking into the guns of enemies in wartime skies.

"That remains to be seen," he said softly. "We'll let Junior be his own judge."

## CHAPTER 10

## SUBSTITUTE HERO

IT WAS NOT very long afterwards that a squad of state police, called by the colonel, took the prisoners away on a charge of kidnapping and attempted murder. Tench was not dead, but he was seriously wounded and unconscious. He would spend time in a prison hospital before coming up for trial.

After that the four Air Force men returned to the car in which Mike's rescuers had arrived. As they were getting in, Mike suddenly thought of something and looked at Johnny grinning. "What took you so long to shoot that gun out of Tench's hand? He took three shots at me before you stopped him. You took a long chance with my life."

"You did it to yourself, Mike," said Johnny. "Fact is we had been waiting on the same street for them to waylay you, we saw the whole thing—had expected it in fact. We followed you and we were listening in. I planned to shoot the moment Tench raised his gun, but you had plans of your own. When you jumped and made a fight for it, I was afraid I'd hit you and it spoiled my aim. I had to wait until I could be sure."

"That's right," chimed in Jack. "Next time you just stand up and be a well-behaved target."

"Not on your life!" said Mike. "How was I to know you fellows were keeping things from me? How is my mother, for instance? Is she really sick? I ought to go see her."

"Your mother's perfectly all right. The telegram was a fake, sent by Tench," said the colonel. "I guess we ought to apologize as well for making you take so long to get here. We have been in town for hours, while you were being stalled in Florida. We had to be sure they'd be waiting for you."

"Hmmm," said Mike, "and now that I'm in my home town, I suppose I won't get to visit my mom and pop after all."

The colonel was driving now. "Look about you, Mike. We're heading for your folks' house now. I am going to let you visit overnight, while the rest of us return at once to Skyhook. Our trap is not finished yet. One part of it remains for you—to keep out of sight and out of contact until Thursday evening or Friday morning."

"So long?" put in Johnny and Jack simultaneously. "But," added Jack, "the orbital flight is Thursday morning! Mike's got to be there to go up."

"Don't worry about it. We haven't been revealing

our real program entirely this time. We still have one rat to catch, and it is essential that he think just what you fellows have been thinking about this Thursday's shoot."

"What do you want me to do?" asked Mike.

The car stopped before Mike's parents' home. It was dark now and the street lights were on. He could see lights inside the house and he was suddenly anxious to get inside and greet his family. But before he left the car, the colonel explained what he was to do. He could visit with his family until the next morning. Early in the morning, he was to leave the house unseen by neighbors. His folks were to say nothing about his visit. Mike was then to go in civilian clothes to the airport at Columbus, to book passage on a commercial liner to St. Petersburg, and to remain there until it was time to return.

"As for you fellows," the colonel said, "I want you to act worried about Mike's absence, talk about it where everyone can overhear you. Van Ness, Holderlin and I will act worried and mysterious about it too."

With that advice, they all shook hands and Mike jumped out of the car.

Wednesday was a busy day at Cape Canaveral, but none of the other astronauts seemed to notice that Johnny and Jack were rather sleepy looking and finding ways of taking naps. They had been up most of the night flying back with the colonel.

Mike's absence at supper back at Skyhook was the cause of several queries. McMahan remarked a couple of times about Mike. "He ought to be back by now," he said. "I don't see how he can make the flight tomorrow if he's missing now. He ought to rest up, be set for it."

Johnny glanced at Jack. "That's right. I'm worried about Mike. There's been no word from him."

"Wonder if something's happened to him," put in Jack, playing up to the part. "I noticed the colonel looking worried. I asked Dr. Van Ness and he just brushed me off."

The other astronauts caught their tone. They ate silently after that. Something was wrong. Where was Mike?

Rod Harger played along with the general mood, but privately he was elated. He tried hard to suppress his good feelings, and when he was alone in his room he all but laughed aloud. He knew what happened to Mike, he said to himself. That was one boy nobody would ever see again, he thought.

"Tomorrow is my day," he whispered to himself, looking over the little room. He glanced at himself in the mirror, poked about his belongings, wondering what would be best to wear under the space suit in the capsule. He turned over some things, and his hand came up with a small package.

He looked at it. It was the thing he had been given by Tench for emergency use as a last resort against Mike.

It was a plastic tube, the size and design of a tube of toothpaste. It was green and it bore the markings, *Vegetable paste. Specially prepared for zero gravity rations.*

Rod had seen others exactly like it, had used them in tests while flying under weightless conditions. This one, he knew, was not what it seemed. It was not a container for food at all. It held an explosive compound. Remove the cap, and once the air got at the chemicals inside, the thing would explode.

"Best get rid of this," he said to himself. He looked for a place to throw it, saw none. He left his room, made his way down to the kitchen which was dark and empty. He glanced around for the garbage disposal can, didn't see it, finally dropped the tube into a box at one corner of the room, not noticing it bounce out of the trash and fall behind onto the floor.

Next morning was the big day, the astronauts knew. The rocket at Complex 34 was ready. The checkout had been going on since before dawn, the actual countdown was due to start in a few hours. Then it would rise, with its capsule, into orbit. The astronauts came down with a bounce to an early breakfast.

Mike was not there, and again they were troubled. The colonel simply shrugged his shoulders. "The flight will go on as scheduled," he said. "We hope Mike will show up in time."

Rod Harger ate swiftly, almost too excited to chew. He knew Mike would not show up.

They went on to the cape. They gathered in the Central Control Building, this time for a briefing. While they waited, Rod kept a careful eye on the time. When he judged that enough time had passed, he left the group, went on down to the locker room.

Here he found attendants waiting with the special pressurized flight suit designed for the rocket riders. At Rod's orders, they assisted him to get into it, fastening the one-piece ventilated pressure suit on him, helping him into his helmet and preparing him for flight. The attendants asked no questions.

When Rod was ready he came out of the locker room to find the astronauts gone. They had preceded him to the pad. He found a car waiting outside, and ordered its airman driver to take him to Complex 34.

Rod sat inside, thinking to himself that his moment of triumph was only a countdown away. This was it. He got out at the blockhouse, and as he emerged Dr. Van Ness and Colonel Drummond came to meet him.

"Hello," said the colonel, "where do you think you're going in that outfit?"

"Why," said Rod, a little puzzled but still sure of himself, "with Mike Mars dead, I knew you had listed me as the next for the flight. I was sure you'd want me to get ready, so the countdown won't be delayed."

"Who told you about Mike's death?" asked the colonel, in a quiet tone of voice.

"Why," said Rod a little confused. "I overheard one of the men at Skyhook whisper it to someone. I don't remember exactly who, but I realized from watching you and the other directors that it must be so. It was a shock to me, sir, but the flight must go on."

The colonel looked at Rod a moment without speaking. "You know then about Mike's sad fate. None of the other astronauts told you about it? Did you tell any of them?"

Rod regained spirit. "No, sir," he said. "I was sure you wouldn't want their spirits upset until after this Atlas shoot."

"But your spirits aren't upset, eh?" asked Dr. Van Ness in a low voice. "You're ready to be a hero in Mike's place?"

Rod became suddenly very uneasy and his heart began to thud. Something was strange here. "It's my duty . . ." he began.

*"I must place you under arrest!"* said Col. Drummond.

"No!" suddenly snapped Colonel Drummond in a powerful and angry voice. "It's my duty to place you under arrest! Mike Mars is not dead and no one ever said he was, either at Skyhook or here. Only someone in the plot to kill him could have believed him dead, and you have just told us with your own mouth who that was—you, yourself!"

Rod panicked then. He turned, as if to try to run, but in that cumbersome outfit it was ridiculous and he stopped. The security guards took him away. What his fate would be a court martial would decide.

At the blockhouse the news spread among the five astronauts clustered there to watch the flight. They were astonished and angry. Then Orin McMahan put the other question, the same one that had tripped up Rod.

"If Mike's not here today, then who is going to ride this Atlas into orbit?"

## CHAPTER 11

## "BERMUDA REPORTS . . ."

COLONEL DRUMMOND didn't answer for a moment, but glanced around the blockhouse watching the intent missilemen at their readings, and looked at the clocks.

A voice, the man giving the countdown, droned out, "T minus forty minutes and counting."

Drummond looked at the five young men now. "This is when the astronaut would be already installed in the capsule. It should be obvious by now that we have not planned on having a living pilot in this flight. Instead, a dummy of human weight and balance has been installed in the capsule out there, and will be the only 'pilot' aboard.

"You see this is actually not the orbital flight itself but a full-scale rehearsal flight. We couldn't chance a human life without such a flight. In particular it should be obvious that if the person who planned and hoped to profit from the sabotage of the earlier Redstone flights ever had a perfect chance to change this rocket, it was now. That is why we had you men working on this Atlas from the start."

"You mean you gave each of us a chance to condemn ourselves in our work?" asked Hart Williams under his breath.

"We apologize to you fellows for the little deception here. But I think you all agree that our plans worked out, even though differently from expectations. Judging from Rod Harger's willingness to go up on this shoot, I would say this rocket has not been sabotaged."

"It could still go haywire. There's thousands of things that can go wrong," said Jack Lannigan quietly.

They fell silent then and concentrated on the countdown. Steadily the time grew closer for the Atlas to take off. Somehow they felt a little letdown that this, which they had worked on so carefully, was not to be the final showdown. But the excitement grew steadily in the dramatic suspense as the minutes ticked by, became a matter of seconds.

The gantry was pulled away, the horns outside blew their last minute warnings, the all-clear was given by the central area officer, the seconds drew down, a finger went down on the button, the Atlas was on its own, the zero second struck, the fires burst from the engines, the silver tower with its air-cabin cargo struggled to rise from the ground, began its slow ascent, moved faster, then onward and upward.

They watched breathless while the calm men in the blockhouse went about reporting. "Steady and rising . . . Boosters complete and jettisoned . . . Leveling on course . . . Burnout . . . Capsule released . . ."

The minutes went by in a pitch of excitement. Now the capsule was moving on its way, high up there beyond the air envelope of Earth, out among the stars. There was a wait and then the first report came in. "Bermuda reports capsule on orbit." A sigh of relief, repeated a little later when the low hum of conversation was broken by the next telemetry station's report from somewhere in the mid-Atlantic. "On orbit and tracking."

Drummond and the five pulled out of the blockhouse then, drove to the Central Control Building and joined the group of engineers and scientists gathered there. For the next hour they listened to the steady return of reports as the capsule, in orbit, circled the Earth for the first time.

They could see the registering of its own automatic reports back to Earth, relayed by the various stations. Then they listened as it returned at last, once around the Earth, passing over Florida again a hundred and fifty miles up and working perfectly.

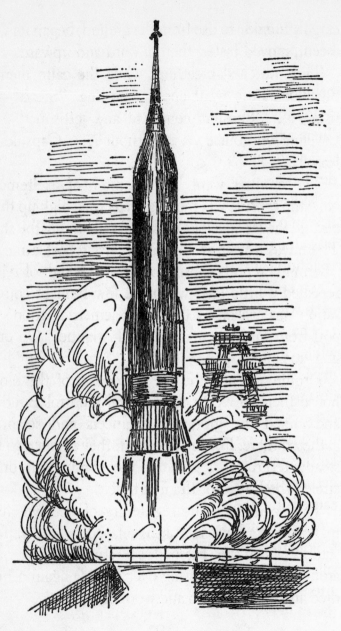

*The silver tower rose from the ground.*

"If Mike had been in there, the trip would have been perfect," said Johnny Bluehawk.

"Oh, give me a chance," said a familiar voice just behind him.

Johnny whirled around. "Hey!" said Johnny, "here's the little man who wasn't there."

"Yeah," said McMahan, "we heard you were dead. You make a pretty lively looking ghost."

Mike smiled, then sobered up. "Let's not kid about it," he commented. "Somehow I'm sorry for Rod. It was an ugly business."

Johnny glanced at the others, then commented, "You keep insisting on seeing the other fellow's side, even when it's so sour. Why do you do it, Mike?"

The sandy-haired young astronaut was silent a while, looking and listening to the reports coming in. Then he said slowly, "I can't help it. I feel that no one is completely bad, not even Rod, except as circumstances make them so. I can understand Rod's motives—it would be a grand and glorious thing to be the first man in space—but personally I couldn't get any pleasure out of it unless I felt I really had earned it."

The serious phase of the test was approaching, as Colonel Drummond now informed them. The capsule was coming around on its second orbit and the attempt would be made to bring it down. "Re-entry is the touchy problem," was the colonel's warning.

The re-entry was to be handled entirely by electronic controls from the ground. They watched the reports of its being slowed down as it came across the Pacific, and listened to the checkout as it began its lowering toward the surface of the Earth. As it passed once again over Florida it was already bucking and heating in the deeper atmosphere. They watched as the minutes sped by in the last critical phase. Down it came over the waters of the Caribbean and the stations there were checking it every second of the way.

Then came the final word. "Parachute sighted," reported a Navy tracker off the island of Puerto Rico. The rest was simple. The rehearsal had been a success.

As the Quicksilver men flew back to Orlando to return to Skyhook, someone remembered to ask when the real first flight would be scheduled.

"Mike Mars," said the colonel, "will take off on Tuesday, in the capsule already checked out atop an Atlas that has been put in preparation the past two weeks at Complex 31. The regular missilemen have been working on it at the same time you were working on today's Atlas."

For those back at Skyhook, the technicians, the regular staff, it had been a slow day and a quiet one. Dr. Van Ness had been at the tracker station at Bermuda, along with the volatile little old woman

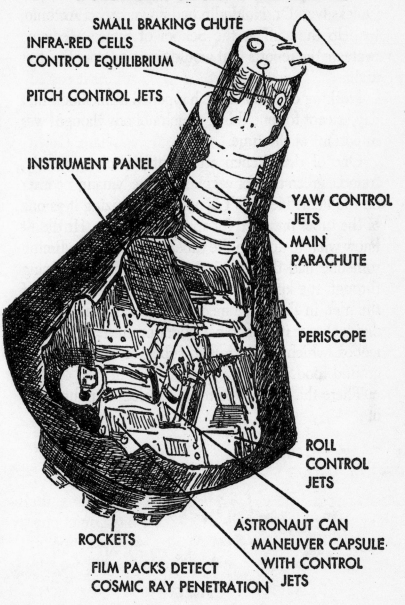

SPOILER TURNS CAPSULE IF YAW JETS FAIL

SMALL BRAKING CHUTE

INFRA-RED CELLS
CONTROL EQUILIBRIUM

PITCH CONTROL JETS

INSTRUMENT PANEL

YAW CONTROL
JETS

MAIN
PARACHUTE

PERISCOPE

ROLL
CONTROL
JETS

ROCKETS

ASTRONAUT CAN
MANEUVER CAPSULE
WITH CONTROL
JETS

FILM PACKS DETECT
COSMIC RAY PENETRATION

who had proven herself so invaluable to Project Quicksilver. Dr. Holderlin had flown to San Antonio, to help the staff at the School of Space Medicine evaluate the reports that would come in from this test flight.

Nothing of importance happened at Skyhook that day, except for one thing, which nobody thought was important at the time.

One of the kitchen attendants, coming in early, found a green tube of vegetable paste lying in a corner on the floor. He didn't open it, recognizing it as one of the tubes prepared for space-flight diets. He didn't know what to do with the tube at first, then, assuming someone had dropped it by accident while passing through the kitchen, the attendant gave it to one of the men in the space medicine office there. This individual took it back to his laboratory and put it in the icebox which held similar tubes of prepared and ground food.

There the green tube rested, sealed, airtight, waiting.

## CHAPTER 12

### "T MINUS ZERO"

THE open framework elevator rose slowly level by level up the red and white painted girders of the towering gantry. Standing on the platform as it rose were three men. One of them was a gray-haired man of rather distinguished appearance, dignified, somewhat stern, but with the faint tracery of lines about his mouth and eyes that betrayed good nature and pleasant humor. At the moment this man was silent, staring out across the sands and scrub brush of Cape Canaveral.

The second man was also silent and he had in common with the first man his age and his dignity. He was a big man and his twinkling blue eyes were a light note in a face framed by a shock of black hair and a black mustache and Vandyke beard. He was looking out through the open bars of the elevator gate at the gleaming silver sides of the object that stood alongside them, held in the metal arms of the giant gantry.

Both men acted as if there was nothing unusual about the third person, the young fellow who stood between them. Strange to say, this chap's eyes also were gazing out across the sands of the Florida cape, fixed on the faint line of blue that marked the edge of the sea. He was dressed all in silver, wearing a form-fitting but bulky suit of metallic material, ribbed along the arms and legs. On his head, concealing his hair, was a white hard-type Air Force helmet with the letters M.A.R.S. neatly printed on the rim and above them the star insignia of the United States Air Force.

This young man was carrying another helmet in his hands, a bucket-shaped affair of metal and rubber and transparent plastic. This was the air-tight helmet that would complete the sealing of his pressure suit and make it a self-contained system, supplying its own air, and maintaining its own interior pressure and temperature.

As the elevator approached the top level the young man's lips moved quietly. Whether either of his escorts noticed this, he never knew. He was repeating something to himself, a little poem he had made up as a boy when he first realized his life ambition was to be a space flier in those days when space flight was still a dream of a few engineers and science-fiction writers.

114

He said softly to himself:

"Michael Mars is my name,
America's my nation,
Space-flying is my game,
And Mars my destination!"

He broke the silence of that ride then by laughing
gently. His two companions turned their eyes on him,
startled out of their own reveries.

115

"You see something funny, maybe?" asked the gray-haired one, the famous Dr. Hugo Holderlin, space medicine expert. "The Earth is such a joke you be glad to leave it?"

Mike smiled and glanced at the German scientist. "Not at all," he said. "Just feeling good."

The other man with them, Merlin Van Ness, nodded to himself. "That's the best news I've heard in weeks," he said. "It echoes my own feelings. Ah, if I were younger . . ."

The elevator came to a stop and the three walked out on the narrow platform. Several men in coveralls and tin helmets were standing there waiting for them. "You did your share," laughed Mike. "Maybe you'll get to go up someday anyway."

They grew silent then as Mike raised his pressure suit helmet and they helped fit it over his head and adjusted it to the rim of his suit's collar. Checking his suit once again, Dr. Holderlin announced that all was set.

They helped Mike climb through the narrow hatch of the orange-painted capsule, poked their heads inside as he slid down into the form-fitting contour seat inside. They assisted him in attaching the various straps and connections which would connect his suit with the system of the space shell and with the electronic records which would make his every breath a matter of knowledge on the ground below.

When all was satisfactory, one of the workmen brought a small box over and with Holderlin's assistance they passed it into the capsule. Mike fitted it into a spot at one side, clicked the box into place. "This contains water in squirt bottles and several squeeze tubes of ground food paste," said Dr. Holderlin. "On your second circuit, in about two hours of flight, I would like you to attempt a meal."

"Can do," said Mike, his face plate still up. "I'll see you all tonight." He snapped shut his face plate, flipped a switch on his panel, and settled back into the body-conforming grip of the capsule seat.

Outside the workmen replaced the hatch and sealed off the capsule. The two directors of Project Quicksilver hastily made a last survey of the outer shell of the capsule, then joined the workmen going down to the ground.

Inside Mike glanced over his panel, looked into the circular disk of his periscopic eye and glanced out the narrow slit above that gave a direct view of the sky. A voice in his earphones called out, "T minus thirty-five minutes and counting."

Mike nodded briefly to himself, set himself to listen to the countdown.

Somewhere outside the rest of his friends were waiting, his fellow astronauts, and those who had worked and cheered them on. To pass the time he checked over their positions.

Dr. Van Ness would be in the blockhouse right here at the pad on Complex 31. Along with him would be Jack Lannigan and Hart Williams.

Colonel Drummond would be at the NASA telemetry station at Patrick Air Force Base down the beach. With him would be Johnny Bluehawk.

Joseph Stacey and Orin McMahan would be on their way by plane to the telemetry station at Bermuda. They would be checking his flight from there

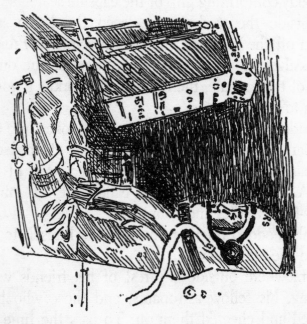

*Mike set himself to listen to the countdown.*

*Vivian Van Ness*

and also be in a position to get to the spot when he
landed, if all was in order.

On the beach, where the rocket's trail could be
seen, would be a little red car with a black-haired
girl at the wheel, Vivian Van Ness out from school
on special leave that day, and with her would be a
little old lady, Amanda Linnet, the only reporter in

the know. Unfortunately, the chipper Mrs. Linnet would not be able to publish a word about what she had seen until possibly years later, for the flight was still top secret.

"T minus fifteen minutes and counting," said the voice from the blockhouse. Mike turned his head, looked over the capsule. It was so small, he thought. Such a limited space, and in a little while it will be the whole world to me. For a time it will be a planet all of its own, a planet with enough air to sustain life for forty-eight hours, a new moon to the Earth system.

Suddenly now he felt thrilled, elated. By gosh, it would be a new world and himself the first man on it. A man-made planet, it would move through the heavens in a true satellite orbit, and Mike Mars would be its population.

This was the first . . . but it would not be the last. Mike again glanced over his instruments. "T minus ten minutes," said the countdown. "Capsule report. Communications, voice?"

"Operational," said Mike crisply. One by one a series of questions was put to him and he answered each precisely and simply. Air, pressure, temperature, fuel gauges, all the readings on his panel were given and proved in order.

"T minus three minutes and counting," said the voice. Mike's lips closed tightly; he settled back inside his suit.

"Missile power," said the test conductor's voice.

"Go," said another voice, checking.

"AMR telemetry?"

"Go," came the answer.

"T minus sixty seconds and counting."

Then, "Range ready light on," came the first voice, followed by, "Final status check."

Rapidly each of the voices replied, "Go," to quick queries on the Atlas pressurization, tanking, water system. "Range operations?" asked the conductor.

"Go," said a different voice, the final word from the Atlantic Missile Range directive itself.

"T minus twenty seconds and counting."

Mike knew that now the water system was on, flushing down in full force the base of the gleaming loaded Atlas. Below him, the electronic systems and relays in the huge missile were clicking into place, the engines readying for their thrust.

"T minus ten seconds and counting."

Cameras would be functioning now, eyes not directed to panels would be glued to the television sets inside the blockhouse. Observers would be raising binoculars at every spot around the cape where men could see the Atlas now wreathed in fumes of boiling liquid oxygen, standing like a tower amid artificial clouds.

"Six, five, four . . ."

The two small engines on the side of the Atlas

would be starting now. Mike let himself relax, allowed a brief smile to cross his face.

"Three, two, one."

Mike rested easily, waiting the first touch of force. In a split instant his eyes crossed the switch set next to his fingers which would activate the escape mechanism. His life might depend on that if something went wrong in the next minute or so.

"Zero."

CHAPTER 13

## "GO, MIKE, GO!"

IN THE orderly precision of the blockhouse, there was a new tension in the air. Jack Lannigan sensed it this time and he knew it was different. Like the other astronauts he had seen flights before; there was a certain excitement—yes, there was always excitement when a big rocket went up—but not the kind of tension that everyone felt now.

He found himself strangely constricted, his throat tight, his body bracing as if he himself were up there, waiting for the final second of thrust. The missilemen at their panels, the operators and conductors of the flight, spoke calmly, their voices betrayed nothing, but he could see that there was lacking that faint touch of ease that had been present before.

These were experienced men, men who had fired the Atlas not once but many times, yet this time was not like all the others. This was it, the moment of human triumph, the moment of a man in orbit, a man who made his own world, who would break apart from Mother Earth and for a brief time ride a new never-before-existing celestial body.

Hart Williams, slender and handsome, was equally silent, and beside him the face of Merlin Van Ness, a man who had seen aviation pioneering, was staring and grim. The seconds slipped by; they heard the words—"a minute," "a half minute," "Twelve seconds,"—and it seemed as if the seconds had hours between them, so keyed up was each man there.

The television cameras showed the sides of the rocket, sheathed now with ice, like a knight in form-fitting armor, this ice the condensed moisture from the air touching the supervold surface of the containers wherein the liquid gases fumed and waited for their moment of fiery escape.

The two little verniers that would steady the rocket ignited, a shock of fire now amid the ice and the gushing waters. A second, then another, and another . . .

There was a puff of smoke, a sudden bellow of white smoke from the base of the rocket. Jack saw it clearly in the television cameras. Jack stopped breathing, as did every man inside the blockhouse; as did everyone whose eyes were fixed on that rocket.

Then there was a blast of fire, a jet of clear, blazing, terrible white light, like a lance of concentrated sun, thrusting down from the clouds of steam, shoving aside the steam for a moment to glare with a brilliant fury that seemed blinding even through the medium of the black and grays of the television.

Far off, those on the observation platform could see the fire too, and everyone stared—three streams of fire from the three mighty Atlas chambers blasting and tearing away at the pad below it, with fury and power that would have destroyed the cement immediately if it had not been for the torrent of water raging against the base.

The rocket began to rise; it snapped the wires that were still plugged into its side, snapped them as if they had never been, and rose against the ground, fought to overcome the terrible weight of its loaded body, of its precious cargo.

For an instant the Atlas seemed to stand on a tiny column of fire, seemed to stand motionless as if having gone up a foot or two it could not make up its mind to go the rest of the way. Then it overcame its hesitation and rose on, rising now, past the single toppling steel frame that had alone held it upright in those final minutes, rising now out of a raging bubbling swamp of steam and smoke that rolled outwards from the pad.

The Atlas was up now, clear in the blue sky, with its bulge of orange on top containing the breathing living body of a young man, Mike Mars, rising on to the heavens on a steady stream of white raging fire.

Outside there was no one who did not know what was happening. The roaring sound coming from the distant pad slammed against every building and car and person for miles around. It screamed like a giant in anger. It was hoarse and howling, and the deafening sound was music to the ears of the rocketmen who heard it. It meant the Atlas was alive, was moving, was up.

Johnny Bluehawk heard it fifteen miles away through the open window, and it was a faint far-off thunder like a storm coming up across the sea. He watched the readings on the panels ranged before him, with Colonel Drummond at his side and the calm efficient men of NASA sitting down checking off the readings as if it were all in the day's ordinary work.

"One hundred feet," said Drummond in a choked voice, "and going good."

"Pressure on the astronaut rising," commented one of the engineers tightly. "Pressure still rising."

The colonel's eyes flicked over that man's panel. It was connected with the electronic registers in the capsule. It told everything that they wanted to know about the pressure of gravity inside the capsule. Four G's pressure now, and the meter was rising.

Mike would be crushed down now, breathing, conscious, but holding on against the greater pressures to come in seconds more, pressures that would squeeze his eyeballs in, thrust his lips away from his teeth, sink in his cheeks, make every breath-taking an exercise in weight lifting.

Johnny, the young Cheyenne, leaned over that board. "Hold on, Mike," he whispered, "hold on," just as if his friend could hear him.

The colonel was watching the gauges and from somewhere came the voice of the test conductor in the blockhouse far away, "Plus twenty seconds."

Only twenty seconds so far, thought Johnny, and it seemed like a lifetime. He could still hear the thunder, but it would fade soon.

Standing up in the front seat of her little red car Vivian Van Ness held a pair of field glasses glued to her eyes and watched a now tiny spark of white fire disappear into the heavens. She was jumping up and down, all unaware of her action, and she was whispering over and over, "Go on, Mike, go on, go!"

And in the blockhouse grown men and youthful astronauts alike were leaping up and down, just like children and hollering the same. Save for the conductor calmly counting down the seconds after firing, and for those whose duties still kept them at their panels, missilemen were acting as they had not acted for many months. Jack Lannigan and Hart Williams were leaping up and down, eyes glued on the television camera that had been swiveled to follow the fast disappearing trace of the rocket.

"Go on, Mike, go on!" they shouted in unison, and the other men, the engineers, the hardened technicians of Cape Canaveral and Complex 31, were yelling the same.

Dr. Holderlin, in the bio-medical laboratories at Patrick's NASA building, leaning over the panels, forgot himself for the moment, forgot his dignity and his gray hairs and was shouting in German as the gauges registered. "Blood pressure still O.K., hurry you demon, hurry! Six G's pressure and rising," he shouted, "Hold on, boy, hold on! You can do it!"

The other space physicians there were smiling and just as tense. They watched and pretended they did not notice their famous superior, acting like a boy again with excitement.

"Go on, Mike, go on!" rang through the block-house now in a chant. You couldn't hear the seconds tick off, the rocket was not visible save as a tiny fast fading dot in the screen, but the electronic records were coming in strong. The astronauts were hopping in anxiety now, the missilemen were waving their hands in rhythm, second by second.

"There it goes!" shouted Jack Lannigan. "The boosters reached burn-out!"

There was a concerted cheer from the men, as the rocket reached its second stage. The two boosters had completed their mission, had burned out, and now were detaching, falling away from the central sustainer rocket.

"Boosters detached," said the countdown voice. "One hundred and thirty seconds and counting."

Now the Atlas would be rising for the final effort, racing at seven thousand miles an hour, speeding up to make the orbital velocity on the power of its main engine. Every second at that pace added greatly to its speed.

"Go on, now, do it, Mike, you can do it!" shouted Jack Lannigan; and Merlin Van Ness, next to him, found himself perspiring with anxiety, muttering and whistling to break the tension.

"Eight G's," muttered Colonel Drummond at Patrick, and Johnny Bluehawk groaned beside him. He knew from experience what Mike must be going through. Every bone aching, every inch of flesh pressing down cruelly, viciously, unrelentingly, his stomach trying to force its way through his backbone, his heart fighting to beat, his breath almost stopped, painfully struggling to force the air through his agonized open mouth.

"Not long now, Mike, not long," whispered Johnny.

In the blockhouse the excitement suddenly died, as if just now the men realized the agony that the Atlas rider was going through. They stood, like statues in a game, watching the seconds count off, watching the speed rise and rise.

It rose fast now, they could see the meters swinging over, and beside them the mileage from the surface. The rocket had long ago turned itself in its orbital direction, was heading out in a slightly northeasterly direction.

Then it was the moment they had all waited for.

There was a click from one of the machines, a stoppage of one register. "Main engine cut off," said the countdown voice, now unexpectedly rising in pitch as if at last he too had decided to get excited.

"Estimated height, one hundred forty-seven," said one of the men, leaning over his panel.

"Speed seventeen thousand, four hundred, by estimate," said another.

"He should be in orbit," said Dr. Van Ness turning to the two astronauts with him. "If the figures check, he's in orbit!"

"Hurray!" shouted the two astronauts, and then the blockhouse took it up and the men were hollering and jumping as if everything had started all over again.

"Now," said Dr. Van Ness sharply. "Let's try to get Mike himself. They must be calling him!"

## CHAPTER 14

## *QUICKSILVER ONE*

SOMEONE was calling. Mike groggily shook his head, someone was calling him. He blinked his eyes. They hurt, but they were all right. Someone was calling him still.

He had not lost consciousness, he told himself. He knew he hadn't. He had managed to see his panels all along; he knew what was happening, but the relief, the sudden relief of coming out of that terrible squeeze that had almost blanked him out! It had been a struggle to keep from going under. The blood had rushed back to his eyes and his face, everything went red and almost black from the release.

Then there had been the flip-flop. The somersault that immediately followed the burn-out of the big sustainer. That hadn't helped. It would have sent him spinning like a feather in the tiny space of the cabin if he hadn't been strapped down. As it was it put a strain on his heart that made him really get a jolt.

Must warn Holderlin about that, Mike thought

then, the first clear thought that came to him. Must tell them not to have that somersault come right on the heels of burn-out, at the moment of weightlessness. The flip-flop could wait a few minutes; be better for the next man to ride on orbit.

Someone was calling. "For goodness sake," Mike said, "I'm dreaming." He wasn't, of course, but he was a little more shaken up than he'd realized. He flipped a switch.

"Quicksilver One," he said, giving the agreed upon call word. "Samson here, and everything is O.K."

There was an audible gasp of relief in his phones. "Bermuda Station here," said a rather faraway voice dimly. "Canaveral Station here," said a much stronger voice right over it and louder. "You are on course, straight and true," it continued. "How are you physically? Did you blank out?"

Mike recognized the voice now as the colonel's. He quickly reported himself as O.K., then briefly admitted his moment of confusion at the end of the burn-out.

"All right, Mike," said the colonel's voice. "Your comment noted. You will be interested to know that the flight was letter perfect. You are proceeding on orbit."

Even as the colonel was speaking his voice began to fade slowly out. Mike leaned forward, his body feathery, weightless by the zero gravity that proved his orbital condition. "You are getting out of range, colonel," he said, and at once added, "Come in Bermuda Station."

The voice which he had first heard dimly came back on the air, and strongly. "Bermuda here. You are receiving very well. We read your signals. Are you weightless?"

"Indeed yes," Mike replied. He looked around the tiny cabin. No damage. He knew from the feel of his body, without any sag in the straps, that he could float around if he unstrapped. He had a feeling of elation now, a heady feeling of pleasure. He even whistled a bit.

"What do you see?" queried Bermuda Station then.

Mike snorted. He had been so busy testing his own reactions, checking the readings on his instruments that he hadn't paid much attention to outside. He looked now, gasped.

Above him he could see the dark black velvet sky of outer space. There was no air around him, or so little that it made no difference. A million million stars shone hard and brilliant, like diamonds that burned with their own light. Though moving easterly, he was himself facing west, traveling backwards, and he could see the sun in his direct plate. He moved a shield of tinted glass across the spot on his window to cut out the blinding brilliance of that disk of white

134

light, and he could see the pockmarks of sunspots on its solar face. He watched the amazing corona that surrounded the sun like a halo of gold and orange and crimson.

He tore his eyes away, looked down at the plate of his periscopic viewer. This gave him a wide angle vision of what was below him and before him in his passage. The Earth was like a vast relief map and he could see the curvature plainly. It was a misty, cloudy relief map, whose contours were often obscured by clouds or misty atmosphere. He could see a greenish dark mass far off that would be the coast of Cuba, and perched above it just as correctly as the maps indicated was the peninsula of Florida. And this was receding visibly, as he watched, to be replaced by an expanse of bluish gray which was the waters of the Atlantic Ocean.

"I can't see you, Bermuda," said Mike, who had been describing all this.

"You won't," said his invisible contact and the voice was fading away now. "You're south of us, and going away." Mike strained to hear this last, then the voice was gone.

He stared down in his seat and watched the ocean fill the view, until all the world below was a slab of ocean, the vast space which dominates the world on which he was born.

One must see it from here to realize that land is the

minority on our planet, Mike said to himself. He opened his switch, called his code name. There was no answer.

He remembered now to open his face plate. He stared again at the stars, mentally trying to identify them. For a while he couldn't, for from space there were so many more than are visible with the naked eye on the ground that he was baffled. The familiar constellations were crowded out by the lights of stars never seen by the unaided eye.

He resorted to his studies, mentally picturing the sky as it should be at that hour from that place. Doing so, he estimated them again, and now he was able to fix one and then another of the brighter stars and suddenly the sky fell into place again and he recognized the constellations, brighter, sharper, somehow more real in the vast infinite depths of the universe.

The sun was dropping toward the horizon slowly but steadily. "A day in ninety minutes," Mike thought. He looked at the ground and he could make out the edge of the night crawling softly across the far eastern waters. He watched it steadily, gave out with his call again.

Another voice came on. "Sargasso Station here," it said clearly enough. "Calling Quicksilver One."

Mike acknowledged, and the new voice went on at once. "Advice from Canaveral and Bermuda observations place you directly on orbit as predicted. Please give us your visual readings."

"Quicksilver One here to Sargasso. Thank you. I knew it would work out all right. Here are my readings."

Mike read off his dials, and as he read, Sargasso Station was quickly fading away. It was a naval vessel somewhere in the middle of the Atlantic Ocean, he knew, and he was not directly over it. Still, better than nothing.

He passed into darkness now, or rather the Earth below did for Mike's manned artificial satellite was always in the darkness of space. The sun sank below, far away in the West, obscured by the bulk of the Earth. The waters changed from gray to black, and Mike could see below only a shadowy darkness with patches of silvery gray that indicated the waters beneath.

He was out of contact for minutes more then. He sat and looked out and realized that even ninety minutes could seem long. He squirmed around, hesitant.

It was so lonely here, he thought. Nothing but empty space above and below. The Earth when in light was somehow at least there, pleasant, suggestive of a place to land. But in darkness, in the night of the Earth, he felt lost.

He shook his head quickly. That was a mental reaction, he told himself, we were warned against it.

Control now, he said to himself, self-control. I am all right, I am on schedule. They know where I am. I will be down on Earth in a few hours, in time for a late supper, he thought.

He pulled himself out of that strange mental funk, realized that a man alone in empty space was in danger of this kind of thinking. Man was made to be a friendly animal, to be among his own, living and talking.

Mike opened his transmitter. "Calling any station," he said. "Quicksilver One calling." Any voice now would be enough to break the strain.

For a while he heard nothing. He repeated his call. Then it came, far away, faint. "Canary Islands Station, hello! Can you hear us, Quicksilver?"

Mike called out, yes, yes, he could. The voice continued faint and far away. "You are still south of us, but we read you. You are on orbit."

Now Mike felt good. "All is well," he said, and read out the readings on his dials. He rather imagined they would not be in touch long enough to hear them all, but it gave him something to do. Then they were gone, faded away into the night.

Desert. Mike reflected on this as he chatted with the man, and in his mind's eye he could see another arrangement of gantries and testing pads, gleaming silvery rockets, and storehouses. Someday, he thought, the British will join us in space; they are well on the road.

Now the dawn was rising over the southern Pacific Ocean and he was crossing toward the Equator again in the final lap of his orbit. Canton Island Station came on, and at long last, in the light of the day, Hawaii.

Mike thought of it as the new day and caught himself. For him a day, but it was the same day as when he had left Florida. He had merely raced around the world and caught up with that day's sunrise.

Hawaii Station said, "Hold on," and there was a clicking. Then another voice came on, a familiar one. "How's it going, Mike?" said the colonel's voice. "Everyone here is cheering for you."

"Glad to hear you, sir," said Mike. "You are being relayed, I take it, through several stations."

"Right," said the colonel. "Now, Mike, do you want to come down, or are you game to go the round twice more, as we had planned?"

"I'm game," Mike said. "Don't bring me down now. I still haven't had my fill of space."

"O.K. then," said the colonel's voice, and was replaced by Hawaii Station again. Mike was held fascinated by the next ten minutes of his ride. He passed Hawaii, swung on over glistening morning-lit ocean, with here and there a touch of cloud reflecting the white rays of the sun. Then at last a coastline appeared and in a few minutes he was over California and heading on toward his original starting point.

America rolled on beneath him. He saw the great stretches of yellowish tan, which were the deserts of the Southwest and then saw them replaced by the greenish browns of the inland areas. At last, having talked with stations along the way, he heard the colonel's voice again and saw the familiar outline of Florida coming into view.

"First lap," he called, and another voice came onto his phones in answer.

"Hi, Mike," said the tones of Johnny Bluehawk. "All the boys are rooting for you. It's been a ball, catching the reports from all the stations who have been relaying your trip. Give our regards to the man in the moon."

"Gee," said Mike, "it's good to hear you from here. Will do."

Dr. Holderlin's voice came on. "Mike," he said. "I'd like you to try to eat a meal during the next orbit. Do you feel up to it?"

Mike laughed. "Now that you mention it, doctor," he said, "I feel hungry. You know, just sitting here can be a bore. Next time I go up I'll take a book."

The doctor's voice did not sound amused. "You may be right. So dig into the picnic basket the next time you are between stations."

"Right ho," said Mike. It was perhaps a half hour later before he got around to taking the space doctor's advice. He was between Bermuda and the Canary Island stations when he reached down and unclamped the lid of his food box. Arranged neatly in two racks were several tubes of food, and the plastic water containers.

Mike unsnapped one of the water bottles, held it to his face, squeezed gently. He squirted the water into his mouth, not letting it get a chance to escape and float around his cabin like bubbles.

He fingered the several tubes of ground-up food in plastic holders like so many toothpaste tubes. He knew they weren't very appetizing, but he was hungry. He fingered a red tube which he knew would hold some kind of meat paste. Then he remembered how his mother had always insisted he eat his vegetables first in order to clean his plate for what he preferred.

Smiling at his childhood recollection, he reached for a green tube, unsnapped it from the rack, held it up. He uncapped the top.

It hissed at him. Startled, Mike looked at the tube. This was strange. This wasn't food; there was an odd chemical odor coming from the tube. The hissing continued and he felt that the outside of the tube was becoming warm to the touch.

He hastily glanced around, but his space was limited. There was a waste disposal unit, and he squirmed in his seat, swiftly opened the trap of it, and shoved the tube inside. He slammed the trap shut and moved with his hand to discharge the tube from the ship completely.

But it was too late. There was a sudden explosion. Smoke gushed from the tiny door of the waste trap and it swung off its hinges. The capsule bounced to the explosion, and there was a crackling noise, a snapping noise, and somewhere a shower of sparks shot out.

Mike swung a hand over his face, and as he did so, he cried out in alarm.

But there was nobody to hear him.

*Mike cried out in alarm.*

# CHAPTER 16

## THE SILENT SATELLITE

JOHNNY BLUEHAWK and Colonel Drummond were having a snack in the telemetry rooms at Patrick's NASA building when the news first arrived that something was wrong. It came in the form of a phone call, which the colonel took. He hung up, white-faced.

"That was Canary Island Station. They report that Quicksilver One passed over them on schedule but that they were unable to make radio contact with Mike. Further they stated that there are no more readings coming in on the bio-medical channels—which means Mike's body connections."

The Cheyenne started to his feet. "That's strange. What do you suppose has happened?"

Colonel Drummond shook his head. "Something irregular. I don't like it."

They stood and stared at each other. The colonel began making calls, checking back with other stations. At Bermuda Station, everything seemed to be all right. What had happened in the interval?

Johnny meanwhile stood and clenched his fists, slamming them together. He felt so helpless. What could he do? Mike was up there, beyond the reach of any human help. There was no way of getting to him —or at least none that would help. It might be possible to send up another Atlas, and another man in a capsule, and it might be possible to arrange for them to intercept, or come close enough for the astronauts to make their own contact—but it would take several days at least to set up such a flight.

The capsule was capable of sustaining life for two days, no more.

"Maybe," said Johnny, "Mike had to disconnect himself and leave the capsule to get on its outside. Maybe he had to check on something. That would account for why he has not answered radio calls and why his body plug-ins have been disconnected."

The colonel nodded. "That's what I've been hoping. I've alerted all the stations to keep an extra careful vigilance, to try for optical tracking if possible. Since Mike will be moving in a nighttime sky now, it may be possible to see him by the reflected light of the sun—at least for a while."

They waited, tense, uneasy, and all up and down the Cape where the astronauts or those in on the top-secret manned flight waited, the word went out. A chill settled on the missile base. Somehow, even those who did not know what was going on sensed it.

The tracker station in the Gulf of Guinea off the southwestern coast of Africa called in at last. They had spotted Quicksilver One. "It was like a tiny moon," they said, as they saw it in their tracker telescopes shortly after dark. "It went by exactly on schedule, still in perfect orbit."

But their calls had gone unanswered. No reply from Mike Mars. No readings from his body attachments. "Was the capsule still intact?" they were asked.

"Yes," was the answer. Telemetry readings were coming in that said the capsule was still at the predicted temperatures, that at least that part of the electronic equipment was functioning.

The colonel had now been joined by Merlin Van Ness and Hugo Holderlin. Johnny Bluehawk found himself unexpectedly present at a full directorate meeting. But they could decide nothing. They could only hope.

They waited, they talked, they speculated. In time Zanzibar Station reported in. The same story. No visual observation this time, but their instruments showed that Quicksilver One had passed over on schedule, a prompt little moon. No answer from Mike, though. Nobody apparently home.

Mike was shaken up when the false tube of food blew up. It had been a cleverly constructed little bomb. It was the kind that would explode as soon as air was released into the highly volatile contents of the container. Inside the tiny capsule, it would have been quite powerful enough to have destroyed the astronaut unfortunate enough to hold it in his hand. Only Mike's prompt action in getting it out of the way had saved his life.

Mike coughed in the smoke that filled the restricted space of the capsule. His air conditioning system was working, however, and very soon the air was clear. He ran a hand over his face, and realized that he had avoided any personal injury. There was a small bruise on the back of his hand, which was nothing.

So that was first—he was alive and intact. He promptly began a personal checkout of the rest of the capsule.

There was a buckled and broken section near his feet, where the waste trap had been blasted. There were dented spots where bits of metal had evidently struck, but no apparent damage.

Mike glanced anxiously at his air readings. The capsule was still airtight. No loss of air pressure detectable. There had been a real possibility of blowing a hole in the skin of the capsule, but in that way his luck still held.

He went over his dials. Heat control, O.K. Periscope, O.K. Telemetry readings, not so good. Several were not functioning. The cables leading from his contour seat, which had passed close to the spot where the bomb went off must have been broken.

He switched on his radio receiver. There was no hum. He joggled it a bit. Still no hum. Nothing. He was cut off. He tried opening his own sender, calling. That too seemed dead.

Mike bit his lip. Now that was bad. The question was could the ground control men still activate the equipment that would put the capsule into his automatic slowdown and re-entry pattern? If they could, then he had nothing to worry about. When the time came, they would simply bring him down and all would be well.

He looked outside. He was entering the night line now, judging from the ocean he could see below. Soon he would be over Africa on the second swing around the world. He knew they could track him. They'd know where he was all the time. But could they do anything about it?

If they could not bring him down, if he could not himself use the secondary set of controls in the capsule which would enable him to take his own command of the vehicle's retrorockets and land himself, then he was doomed. He would circle the Earth again and again, for days and weeks and perhaps months, a shell of metal containing the body of a foolhardy young man who had challenged space and lost.

Someday it would come down of its own. The

steady friction of even the tiny amounts of air would gradually slow the little man-made moon and bring it closer and closer to the Earth. Then it would become hot and finally at last it would plunge down, a burning meteor that someone might see for a moment and think a falling star.

That would be the end of Mike Mars.

He gritted his teeth. Not while he could do anything about it, he said to himself. "Michael Mars *is* my name," he said in a mood of defiance.

He detached himself from the contour chair, floated lightly upward. "America *is* my nation," he quoted the next line, and reached under the panel for the small case of instruments. Opening it he took out wrench, screwdriver, pliers.

"Space-flying *is* my game," he said loudly, as if daring anyone to deny it. He rapidly began to unscrew the top of the instrument panel, finished, then carefully lifted it up.

"And *Mars* my destination," and he added, "And I won't settle for less!"

He studied the exposed wires, but they were intact. Somewhere his radio connections were severed. He'd trace them, and he ran over the wiring of the capsule in his mind. He'd been working on this tin space can too long not to know every part of it. He mentally pictured the area of the explosion, jotting down in his mind every wire and line that passed through it.

Yes, he thought, the radio connections are broken there.

But to fix them he'd have to either unscrew the contour chair and get under it, or go outside and open a panel from there. The problem of getting the contour seat out was too difficult; there wouldn't be enough space for him to get around in. There just wasn't room enough. So the thing to do was to get outside.

He snapped shut his face mask, went over his pressure suit carefully. It was airtight, self-operating. It was, he knew, a space suit. Now it would get its first real space workout.

He pushed aside the instrument panel, opening the way to his escape hatch. He wormed up it, unscrewed the holding pins, waited a second. When he got it open, the air inside the capsule would pop out, vanish. He had no choice. He shoved.

Tightly wedged in the narrow hatch he himself was not pushed through by the sudden explosion of air. And then he was poking his head out.

He looked into the blank emptiness of space. He looked into black sky, dotted with a myriad stars, and for an instant he felt giddy, with a sensation of looking down into an abyss that had no bottom.

He quickly gained control of his imagination. Not down, but up, he thought, in relation to the Earth,

154

but he could feel then the reality that in space, in free fall, there is no up or down.

He hooked a belt ring on his suit into a catch outside the hatch, slid himself out and onto the bottle-shaped surface of the little space shell. He resolutely shut his mind from the scenery beyond, the dark bulk of the Earth beneath him, the Moon off to one side with its ugly ominous craters, the stars waiting for him to drop.

He slid down until he was over the panel he sought, and, taking his instruments in hand, began to open that section of the shell to get at the wiring.

## CHAPTER 17

## *DECISION AT CANAVERAL*

THEY came to a decision at Canaveral at the time that Canton Island Station, in the Pacific, reported the capsule's passage.

"He will be over Hawaii soon," said Van Ness. "If we start his deceleration at the right moment when he is between Hawaii and the Coast, we will be able to bring him down automatically, just as we had planned. We will not wait for a third orbit of the planet. I suggest that we make the effort to bring Quicksilver One down on the second lap."

The other two directors nodded. Johnny Bluehawk sat silently, listening. He was still nervous with the desire to do something, and the dreadful feeling that there was nothing to be done. But he wouldn't have left that room for anything.

Colonel Drummond answered the phone again. "Canton Island reports," he said when he hung up, "that now the telemetry readings show no temperature inside the capsule. No air pressure. The capsule

157

is apparently empty. Some electronic equipment is still operating though."

The other two looked at the colonel, then glanced at Johnny. His ruddy skinned face had become unusually pale. Was Mike Mars dead?

"We will proceed to activate the retrorockets at the correct time," said Van Ness. The colonel took the phone, gave the necessary instructions.

Mike Mars, clinging to the outside of the capsule, could know nothing of this. He was busy splicing wires, working to get at loose ends, to make patch-up connections. The mess was pretty bad here, he could see, and it was hard and slow working with thickly gloved hands under the eerie conditions of space.

He paid no attention to time nor to where the capsule was in its orbit. None of these things mattered until he could get his repairs done. It did not occur to him that if the attempt was made to fire his slowdown rockets from the ground while he was out there that it might cause his death. A sudden drop in speed of the capsule and he would be thrown off, to be lost in space, wandering in orbit to die in a matter of hours.

So he went on working, and the capsule passed over Hawaii Station's range and the seconds ticked away at Canaveral and Dr. Van Ness stood with his finger on a button that would trigger the impulses from the California High Range Station and start the capsule's rockets firing.

Dr. Van Ness brought his finger down as the second hand came to the marked moment on the big wall clock. Johnny watched and he saw the button go down. This was it, he thought, and the room was in silence as they waited.

Minutes went by. Then finally the California trackers called in.

The object known as Quicksilver One was still exactly on orbit. It had not slowed. It was not descending toward the Earth. It was still up there, still traveling at nearly eighteen thousand miles an hour, still a satellite of this planet.

The four in that control room in Florida looked at each other. "We have lost all ground control," said the colonel, and he felt even as he said it that it was too obvious. Things like that should not be mentioned.

"Mike must be there," said Johnny suddenly. "He must be. I know it. He'll bring it down himself. Wait and see."

The colonel looked at him. "That's our only hope now. If he does bring it down, it could be anywhere in the world now."

"Then let's at least get ready to meet him wherever he comes down," said Johnny, talking swiftly, trying to make himself believe.

*Johnny dashed out with desperate energy.*

"Let's do that," said Merlin Van Ness then. "I think the boy's right. We've got to have faith. Let's get a plane ready, able to take off anywhere. If he comes down, he's going to need help fast."

"Can't harm," said the colonel. He phoned Base Operations. A little later, after some conversation, he turned to the others.

"They've got an F-104B coming down to Patrick now. It'll be here and ready on the flight line in a half hour. Johnny, get ready to take it up, with me. I don't know where we're going, but if we hear the capsule is coming down, we'll be off."

"Good," said the Cheyenne. He dashed out, filled with desperate energy. He didn't know what good it could do. He was pinning his faith on Mike and the unknown, but at least he could be doing something. He could be standing by, somewhere, sometime, somehow.

He ran all the way to Base Operations. Above him the sky was twilight purple. The sun was setting.

## CHAPTER 18

## *POINT OF RE-ENTRY*

CONCENTRATING on the job, holding pliers in clumsy hands and working under the uncertain, steadily shifting light of an unshielded sun in a jet black sky, Mike lost all sense of time. He clung grimly to his task, slowly splicing wires, trying to separate those whose fused condition indicated short circuits, pulling out some, trying to run new connections with pieces of others.

He paid no attention to himself, relying on his suit's inner system to maintain his body heat and pressure, without which he would speedily die. He was conscious of warmth on that part of him directly in the rays of the sun, and he tried to shift himself every now and then to relieve that special radiation from one area and let it work on another.

When, at last, he studied his patchwork and saw that there was nothing else he could do, that he had done all possible to restore what was restorable in the delicate electrical system, he replaced the metal panel, screwed it back on, and worked his way back into the narrow hatch of the capsule.

Feet first he pushed himself into it, then, holding on, he worked the hatch back on, bolted it tight. He was careful not to disturb the parachute tower, which was vital to his descent. He worked himself back into the narrow space of the cabin, replaced the instrument panel over the hatchway, floated himself into the contour seat, and belted himself down, plugging the telemetry wires back into his suit.

He looked at the dials. There was an improvement. More of his telemetry readings were functioning, and that was to the good. His ground control system was still dead, though, and that was bad. He switched on his radio, and at the same time began to study the scene below him on the disk of his periscopic sight.

He was over land. That was interesting. He studied the details, and he was thankful for the many long hours he had spent at Langley and Skyhook on terrestrial geography. In spite of a number of cloud formations and misty areas, he could see the expanse of the American Southwest—part of Mexico, the recognizable outthrusting of Lower California, the desert areas of New Mexico, and Arizona.

He calculated quickly and realized he had been out on the surface longer than he'd thought. What of those below?

His earphones were humming. He leaned forward.

The radio was restored. He could hear static, a carrier wave somewhere. Then a voice came on, faint but distinct.

"Calling Quicksilver One. White Sands Station calling Quicksilver One. Standing by."

Quickly Mike flicked his sender switch. It went over, but the dials registered nothing. He heard no click. He called out quickly, but even as he spoke he knew his sending system was still dead. It had been permanently shorted. He repeated his call, and flicked over the incoming channel.

All he heard was White Sands, New Mexico, fading away and repeating endlessly its same hopeful code.

Mike gritted his teeth. He kept the band open. He sat there, waiting for the minutes to pass, watching the planet roll by beneath him, Arizona, western Texas, northern Mexico. Another voice came on, growing in volume.

"Randolph Station calling Quicksilver One."

Mike nodded. That was San Antonio, Texas. He heard it call several more times, repeating its signal. Then a new voice came on:

"Quicksilver One. If you hear me, listen carefully. Your present position and speed follow."

Mike listened. He picked up a pencil snapped to a holder on the side of the instrument panel, jotted down the numbers as they were given him on a pad also built into the capsule system there.

The voice went on. "If you can, you are to commence re-entry at your own discretion. Proceed at will. Use your own judgment. We are tracking you all around the world. Any shift in your motion will be noted. Attention Quicksilver One. We will repeat the previous figures."

San Antonio went on, though already it was fading out. But Mike had the figures and he studied them carefully.

He checked his clock. It was still working accurately. He studied his position, ran over the orbit that he would follow during the next ninety minutes.

It was still airless within the shell. The air that had escaped once he opened the hatch could not be replaced. He had at best but a few more hours of life left to him now, unless he could find a means of replacing his air, not to mention feeding himself. He realized he was thirsty again, but thrust the thought from his mind. There was no way to satisfy that thirst while he was unable to open his face plate.

He felt that he dared not wait too long before beginning descent, and yet, when and where?

He rode on, lost in thought and deep in calculations as to his re-entry. He heard Eglin Station come in on the Gulf of Mexico coast. It repeated exactly the same message as Randolph. That faded to be replaced almost immediately by Canaveral.

He heard the colonel himself repeating the mes-

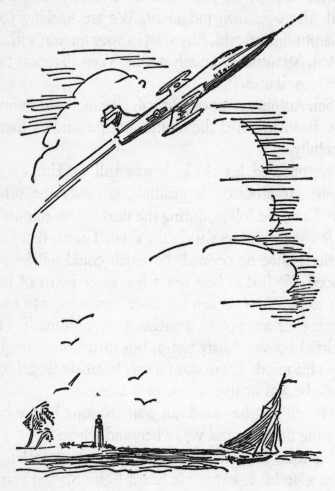

*The* Starfighter *roared across the Atlantic.*

sage. Mike listened, hunched in thought. He looked below. He was crossing the nightline belt now, which had crept across the Atlantic and was touching the coast of North America. In a few more minutes, the Earth was beginning to assume a crescent appearance beneath him as he traveled over into the area of the world lying in shadow away from the sun.

Where should he choose to come down then, traveling as he was in darkness? It would not be good to come down unseen, for his chances of rescue, slim enough, would be far lessened by a descent in darkness.

This meant he had to calculate his return to come down into sunlight. The earliest would be at the sunrise zone or a little beyond it.

He checked over the stations, saw what he must do. The rest was waiting.

He sat it out, and he heard Sargasso Station come in and their figures checked with his. He waited now in growing tension, and at last he heard the call of Canary Islands Station.

He had worked out his moment for action. Now he placed his hands on the studs of his firing buttons, watched the minutes and seconds click off on the panel clock.

Below him the Earth was in darkness. There would still be water beneath him. In a matter of minutes, it would be land, the bulge of northwest Africa, the slide past in darkness of Guinea, and Ghana, and Nigeria and the other new nations of the World. The clock ticked away the seconds. He counted to himself, like a countdown, watching. "Thirty, twenty-nine, twenty-eight . . ."

His finger rested on his retrorocket button. Then, counting himself down to zero, he pressed the button, prayed it would work.

He felt himself jar forward in his seat, held back by the straps. He yelled aloud with relief. The rockets built into the nose of the capsule were firing, blasting away. They were small solid fuel rockets, not very powerful as rockets go, but they were quite enough to slow down the little light capsule of a moon. Slow it down enough to make it lose its orbital speed, make it begin to fall toward the ground below, to slide down in a long dragging glide, breaking its circular orbit until one end of its arc rested on the ground.

Mike pitched and pulled against the straps and the rockets blasted away for ten seconds until their fuel was exhausted. He settled back again, and his weightless condition was gone. He felt a pull, a slight pull but a definite one. The rocket was under the influence of gravity. It was beginning to come down. He braced himself again, for he knew that the worst was yet to come.

Back at Canaveral, the phone rang in the room where the three Quicksilver directors were holding their tense vigil. Merlin Van Ness picked it up, listened a moment.

The colonel watching him saw the bearded scientist's face light up, saw him suddenly seem charged with electricity. "What is it?" said the colonel getting to his feet as if stuck with a needle.

Van Ness hung up. "Gulf of Guinea Station reported that Quicksilver One has changed its speed. It was late coming over them and it is coming down. Mike's still there, still in control and it's coming down!"

The colonel leaped to the big map on the wall. "Where?" he said. "Where will he land?"

Van Ness pointed a finger at the spot. "There. That's the spot he's heading for!"

The colonel shot out of the room, leaped into a

waiting staff car, and raced through the evening to the flight line. He jumped out, ran to Base Operations to get into his jet-flying suit, his G-suit, parachute, oxygen mask and helmet. He put them on faster than he ever had in his life, and dashed out again. On the field, the silvery F-104B Starfighter was already tuning up, and another helmeted flier in the forward cockpit was looking at the colonel impatiently.

The colonel made the plane, scrambled up the ladder, slipped into the seat behind Johnny Bluehawk. "Where to?" said Johnny breathlessly.

"Zanzibar," gasped the colonel. "Puerto Rico first to refuel. Then down the Atlantic Range."

The silvery superfast jet gunned forward, swung onto the airstrip, and then roared away into the nightening sky.

## CHAPTER 19

# THE PIRATES OF ZANZIBAR

THE capsule bounced. Mike was jarred in his straps, knocked breathless for a second. He clung to the arms of his form-fitting chair, braced himself. Once again, a jarring bounce, followed rapidly by another and another.

He was hitting the atmosphere, bouncing into it like a rock skimming the surface of a pond of water. The capsule was bounding off the heavier atmosphere it was encountering, bouncing each time, sinking a little lower, then the bouncing stopped.

Mike held on. There shouldn't be any more of those jolts, but now the heating would start. The capsule was entering the thicker regions of the air envelope surrounding the Earth. Though it was still dozens of miles up, and that atmosphere was far too thin to breathe, it was thick enough to heat the surface of a body entering it at the thousands of miles an hour at which the capsule was still traveling.

The capsule would slow down steadily as it encountered the drag of the air, and as it did so that self-same friction would cause the outer surface to heat up.

The base of the capsule, the wide curved bottom of the tubular vehicle, was designed to absorb the greater part of that heat. It was a curved heat shield, and it would take the brunt of the pounding and air friction. Gripping his seat, watching his periscopic view and glancing occasionally through the narrow slit of his window, Mike could see wisps of smoke racing past, and he knew the specially resistant paint that coated the base of his capsule was already afire, burning and peeling off.

He had experienced this with the re-entry of the rocketship X-15, it did not scare him now. He watched the gauges that indicated the temperature of the outer shell and the inside shell. The first was rising, very rapidly. The second was also going up, enough so that if the tiny cabin space had been filled with air, Mike might now be very uncomfortable indeed. It was then he realized that there had been at least one advantage to his little disaster—by emptying the air within the capsule he had given himself an additional protection against the transmission of heat from the shell.

His suit should hold up, true, but who could say what strains it had not already endured during his work on the outside surface, in the extreme conditions of empty space.

He looked below. It was still night, and he mentally calculated his position. He must now be coming down on a descending curve over Tanganyika. He squinted into the darkness below him. It should be close to dawn, he knew. A faintly gleaming area passed beneath him, reflecting the stars in streaks of glinting light. "Lake Victoria," he murmured to himself, adding in afterthought, "I hope."

The ground below was lightening softly as he approached the slowly moving line of the sunrise. He could see the sun from where he was, on the horizon, its corona already obscured by the blue of the Earth's atmosphere. He was coming down, coming down.

The heat began to recede now, judging from his gauges. He breathed a sigh of relief, watched his altitude carefully. He was over a plateau, wooded plateau and rolling plains, and lions down there would be rising in the first aurora and stirring uneasily, and herds of wild animals would be looking about from slumber, ready to flee or forage for food depending on what jungle news the new day would bring.

The ground was coming closer and he could see the outlines of it taking shape as the sun's rays struck the surface at last. He was skimming along, still high, still descending in a long arc, and he could see the coastline appearing beyond.

As he finally passed the line that marked the coast of Tanganyika, Mike touched a button. The small drogue parachute above him opened up. The capsule quivered as it took hold, shook, then became much steadier. The quivering which Mike had been trying to ignore during the previous period of fall was lessened.

He saw that he was passing over land again, an island off the coast, and he could faintly make out clusters of white dots which must have been towns and areas of green fields which were cultivated orchards. He was coming down now, and he watched, hoping he had not miscalculated and come down on land.

But the other edge of the big island was approaching, and as he neared it, his altimeter registered ten thousand feet; he touched his controls. The capsule jolted and seemed to come to a swaying halt.

His main parachute had opened. A giant sixty-foot wide orange-and-white striped affair, it had blossomed into existence above his tiny metal vehicle.

His descent stopped, and he felt himself swaying beneath the giant chute. Mike knew he was still coming down, and fast enough, but now at a rate which was under control and similar to many test drops he had made during his training.

He was over water. He could see the gentle waves

*The capsule was coming down over water.*

of the Indian Ocean glistening in the rays of the early morning sun.

The capsule struck the water. There was a jarring shock, and Mike held onto his seat by sheer force. Somewhere beneath Mike there was a whooshing noise; that would be air leaving the impact bag which was built into the capsule just for the purpose of taking up some of that shock.

Then he was down. The capsule rocked back and forth. From below he heard a dim and distant thud. That was an underwater bomb, shot down several hundred feet into the water to explode as a signal to trackers.

Mike could hear the waters slapping against the sides of the little metal shell. He could also hear a hissing noise from above him and a gurgling sound near his foot.

He hastily unstrapped his seat belts, unplugged his suit connections, went to work releasing the hatchway again. As he did so, the hissing increased alarmingly. Air was getting into the near vacuum of the capsule from somewhere, and glancing down he could see that the base was already filling with water—the break was not airtight, nor, evidently, was the hatchway any longer.

He worked in haste now, unscrewing and setting aside the instrument panel, opening the entry to the hatch, working his way up to it, and unscrewing the little circular escape hatch. It popped open with a windy boom. He reached back, unpacked his little rubber life raft, hauled it up and tossed it out. Squeezing through, he left the capsule, slid down its sloping side, pocked with blisters and burn marks, and hit the water.

With a couple of strokes, buoyed up by his airtight suit, he reached the little raft and clambered up on it.

Perched on his bobbing rubber boat, he opened his face panel. The air that hit him was good. He breathed deep. There was the water smelling faintly of salt and fish, and above it all there was a curious sweetish odor that reminded him of cooking and of bakery shops.

He sniffed, and he felt his mouth watering. He was hungry all right, but what was that tantalizing odor which seemed to hint of goodies? It was on the faint breeze from the land.

He looked around him and he could see the faraway coast, lined with palm trees. There was a metallic orange color surrounding the boat. He knew what that was. The capsule had discharged that fine powder as a signal to airplanes that might be seeking it.

He twisted back to look at the capsule. It should be flashing a light, should be sending automatic radio signals. The latter would not be working. The light wasn't working either and the capsule was already settling deep in the water. He watched it and in another few seconds it tipped gently, there was a sudden glubbing noise, and it vanished, sunk beneath the waters.

Now he settled back on his rubber raft. He ought to start paddling toward the land, he thought, but for the moment he rested, just taking in the peaceful scene. So this is Zanzibar, he thought. A name in postage stamp albums, and that's all I really know about it.

Off the coast, perhaps ten, maybe fifty, even a hundred miles away there would be a United States Navy vessel, equipped with telemetry and delicate astro-

*Mike saw a strange looking craft approaching.*

nomical equipment. That would be Zanzibar Station. They must know he was down here, and he felt sure it would not be long before a little Navy plane would be around hunting for his dye-mark in the water. He glanced across the horizon, but saw nothing.

Then he heard a rhythmic *boom-diddy-boom* coming from somewhere. He looked out along the northern horizon. The coastline spread far to his west, a faint tracery of green trees and white sand. To the north was sea. He watched, and finally he saw a dark spot approaching.

The drumming was coming from there. He watched carefully, then waved his hands. It was a boat, surely, but why the drumming?

He sat back as it came in sight, and the closer it

came, the more uneasy he felt. It was a sailing boat, with high prow, low sides. It had a big slanted crescent-shaped red sail hanging full on a single high mast.

He could see the bearded faces of men standing in the prow looking his way. Their heads were swathed in white cloth, and in the stern of this strange boat from a distant barbaric past there was a black figure beating on a big drum. *Boom, boom, boom-diddy-boom.*

The wild Arab craft swung toward him. He swallowed, waved a hand. They looked like pirates, like ancient slavetraders, like sea-bandits, he thought. He could see wicked curved daggers in their belts; he could see sharp eyes over hooked noses, some were Arabs and some were black men, but one and all they looked fierce.

The black man in the stern pounded on his drum like a wild man, and the booming echoed in Mike's ears as the dhow with its wicked scarlet sail closed in to pick him up.

He realized then just how empty-handed he was. He was unarmed. Nobody had ever suggested he take his automatic along. He was without a passport. And he had only a few dollars on him.

The piratical vessel with its mad drummer swung alongside, and many hands, long-fingered and dirty-nailed, reached for him.

## CHAPTER 20

## HALF A WORLD AWAY

IT PROVED to be one of the most grueling flights Johnny Bluehawk had ever made. Flying a high-speed jet plane is an exhausting task, for it calls for alertness, speed of action, and ability to judge at all times the probable future course and controls of the plane. Flying such a plane around half the world could be exhausting under normal conditions. Considering that it was already evening when Johnny and the colonel took off they faced the additional hazard of sleep. Sitting immovable in a cockpit riding through the darkness of night with nothing to see save the dimly lit meters on the dashboard is an easy way to put yourself to sleep.

It speaks wonders for Johnny's top-notch physical condition that he did not nod at the controls. As for the colonel, well, frankly he did snore through the last half of the long trip.

The F-104B, loaded with extra wingtip fuel tanks, had to break its flight with put-downs every fifteen hundred miles, more or less. It was down the Atlantic Range first. A refuel at Ascension Island in the distant South Atlantic, the farthest little point on the Missile Range was their farewell to the New World. Then a jump across to a NATO field on the coast of West Central Africa. At this point, the colonel insisted that Johnny take an hour's nap. After that, the plane refueled, the sun already risen, the silver plane took off once more.

Across Africa in daylight . . . Johnny would have loved to have made that trip close to the ground, at a comfortable speed. He would have seen sights that explorers had struggled for years to see. But he had only one sight in his mind . . . and flying six miles up at over a thousand miles an hour, sightseeing was better left for others.

They made Nairobi in the high plains of Kenya in time to join the officers of the Royal Air Force Base there for afternoon tea. There, also, they left their USAF plane and transferred as passengers to an RAF transport plane. It seems, the commander explained, that the Sultanate of Zanzibar simply had no facilities to land a high-speed jet interceptor.

They arrived at the airport in Zanzibar an hour or so later. As they disembarked from the two-prop transport, the colonel caught sight of a small plane, with U. S. Navy markings, parked on the field. He and Johnny went over, inquired.

They found the pilot. He was a young naval flier, and, as they had guessed, he was from the vessel that had made up the NASA link. "We've been searching for your man all day," said the lieutenant, "and we haven't located him."

They had found the dye mark in the water and had accepted the fact that the capsule had sunk. But there was no sign of Mike Mars, his rubber raft, or any evidence as to where he was. They had sent a launch to the spot, landed men on the coast and hunted, hoping that Mike had paddled in to the sandy shore. They had found no sign.

Now the pilot had flown his ship's captain into Zanzibar airport to alert the native officials. "Come on along," the pilot said. "I'm to meet the captain outside the Secretariat Building near the Sultan's Palace. He's been organizing a search."

They found a waiting car and they drove into the city. To Johnny—and to the colonel—Zanzibar was a mystery, a place of exotic wonder. They drove through crowded streets and noisy Arab markets, they maneuvered through incredibly narrow passages and finally they came out along the peninsula facing the sea on which the old stone city of Zanzibar was built.

The naval captain was waiting for them, and at his suggestion they found a table in an open restaurant attached to an English residents' club.

The captain outlined the search which was being

made for the capsule's astronaut. They had had to keep secrecy, yet alert as many searchers as they could. It had been awkward, but planes from the RAF were still searching the waters, for both the astronaut and the capsule.

They sat there, the four Americans, and they could see out over the crowded harbor, watching the many strange ships working their way into port as the time of sunset was approaching. Johnny wondered what had happened to his friend. Where could Mike Mars be?

He twisted in his seat and looked at the others. He sniffed. There was a strange interesting scent in the air. It smelled like a bakery, or perhaps something more enticing.

He'd smelled plenty of other smells in Zanzibar, the kind of smells you would expect from an old old city without much plumbing, where unusual tropical trees grew. There was a smell of rotten eggs from somewhere—he couldn't place that—and the smell of cooking, and oils, and growing things. And it was a noisy town too. Drums, a lot of drumming in the African quarters, and Arabic music from many windows and from the native eating places, much of which came from scratchy records on old machines. There was yelling and the noise of voices in unknown languages.

But over all was that strange scent. "What is that

I keep smelling?" Johnny asked. "Sweet, mouth-watering?"

The captain sniffed. "It's cloves. Zanzibar is a spice-growing island. Most of the world's cloves are grown here. Look down there."

He pointed a finger down to the docks below them. Johnny looked and he could see piles of sacks there. Men were loading them on some of the curious slant-sailed ships that waited at the docks. He raised his eyes and looked out over the water.

There were other ships coming in, the odd-shaped dhows of Africa, with their red or yellow crescent sails, their wild-looking crews, their drummers that seemed so much a part of their thinking—a type of sailing that had continued unchanged since before the days of King Ramses of ancient Egypt.

Johnny saw a glint of silver on one such ship now plying its way into the harbor. He stared sharply, stood up. There was one among the tiny figures lean-ing over the prow who was not wearing a white Arab burnoose; one whose hair was sandy and not the ex-pected black of those regions.

"Hey!" he yelled. "Look! Look! Can that be . . . it is! It's Mike!"

The other three jumped to their feet, gazed out at the incoming dhow. Then, with one accord, the four of them ran around the outside of the club, and dashed madly down the old stone stairs leading onto the quay.

They reached the end of the pier like four madmen; and the black men working there, and the white-robed Arabs haggling over the sacks of cloves, stood aside and looked at them in wonder.

The red-sailed ship came closer and now Mike caught sight of them. He waved a hand and tried to call, but he couldn't be heard over the noises of the harbor.

It was only a little while later that he was sitting with them all, back at the table facing the waterfront, and gulping down a good supper.

"And so," Mike said, between bites, "they hauled me out of the water. I was scared, you can bet. They sure looked like a bunch of pirates. But they turned out to be quite nice. They were just traders. They sailed all the way down to Zanzibar from Oman in Arabia. They were carrying a load of roofing tiles, of all things.

"I couldn't find any among them who could speak English, but we managed to make ourselves understood. They weren't going to be hurried either. They sailed slowly around the coast of Zanzibar, made a couple of stops in small villages where they traded a bit, and it's been all day before they finally got to Zanzibar city itself.

186

"And oh boy was I glad to see you! That drummer was about to drive me out of my mind!"

The others laughed. The colonel beamed at Mike shoveling food into his mouth, still bright-eyed, and undisturbed by his experiences in space. There were more space experiences ahead for Mike Mars. But there'd be time enough to tell him about them when they got back to Skyhook. Meanwhile let the two boys celebrate and see the scenes. You don't get to Zanzibar every day, he thought.

As for Mike, he was aware that he'd come up another rung in the ladder to space. This had been a big step too, and it would bring him a long way toward the day that the moon would be ready for a human footprint. All space was waiting for humanity, and Mike Mars was ready to be there among the first.

c28